THE GOLDEN APPLE

MICHELLE DIENER

🌸 Formatted with Vellum

ABOUT THE GOLDEN APPLE

Kayla's world has been turned upside-down...

Her father has made her the prize in a deadly, impossible tournament, and Kayla has retaliated in the only way she knows how; by choosing her champion beforehand. But taking control of the outcome changes the game completely, and when the real reason behind the strange test becomes apparent, Kayla realizes not just her life, but her entire kingdom is at stake.

Rane's honor is torn in two...

In order to save his brother, Rane will do whatever he has to—including deceive and betray a princess. He knew nothing about this tournament would be easy, but Rane is forced to see it through to the end, or leave his brother at the mercy of their enemy.

Now their fates are entwined, and they must venture into the deep, dark forest together...

Kayla and Rane are bound to one another, enchanted to complete the task set by the sorcerer behind her father's strange test. Their journey leads them through the heart of the dangerous Great Forest, to complete a quest neither wants any part of. But the sorcerer forcing them to do his will may have miscalculated, because no-one comes out of the Great Forest unchanged. No-one.

CHAPTER 1

The laughter rising from the festivities below was not at her, although it felt like it was.

Kayla threaded her fingers together on her knees and closed her eyes anyway, trying to block out the sounds of merriment.

She was part of the entertainment, and her father's subjects were throwing themselves wholeheartedly into the spirit of the occasion.

Whereas she . . . if she had been clamped naked into the stocks, she could not have felt more exposed, more vulnerable. More disrespected.

Even knowing today was coming had not prepared her for sitting high above a shouting, laughing crowd—merry with holiday fever—in a gilded chair on top of a glass mountain.

She opened her eyes again and watched the fair-goers move below her, skirting the mountain as they talked, ate and drank. More a mystery than how a glass mountain came to be in the jousting field was their acceptance of the mountain at all. It had appeared in the night a few days ago, and now it glittered and flashed in the early morning sun, blinding the unwary.

Was she the only one who wondered at the power it would take to create something like this?

It stood perhaps three stories high, almost as high as the castle itself, but although its peak did not reach the height of the castle towers, it squatted malevolently beside her family home, dominating it.

But if the mountain made no sense, what made the least sense of all was that her father would do this to her.

Auction her off to the boldest adventurer to try his luck here today.

And yet he had.

He'd stuck her up on this crystal monstrosity like the cherry on top of a cake. Her dress wasn't red, though. It was virginal white.

And that color was no longer appropriate for her. Not after last night.

The breeze blowing the sounds of the fair and the aroma of cooking pies up to her suddenly felt cool against her heated cheeks.

As if it could sense her thoughts, the golden apple in her lap throbbed, heating the skin of her thighs through her thin skirts.

She looked down at it with loathing. A distorted image of her face looked back at her through the shine. As distorted as her world had become since her father embarked on this mad course.

She lifted her hand, hovered it over the apple. Her father had worn gloves when he placed it in her lap, just before she was lifted up the glass hill.

"Don't touch it," he'd said. Then he'd walked away, her obedience a foregone conclusion.

She wanted—wanted so badly—to toss it. To throw it, as far and as hard as she could, away from her.

She hesitated, just a moment, then closed her hand over it. And cried out. A light leapt from the apple to her palm, the pain hot, intense. She let go, and immediately the light disappeared. The pain lingered, a throbbing reminder, and then faded away.

She stiffened her spine against the tears clogging her throat and pricking her eyes. She had given away her innocence last night, so pride was the only thing she had left.

No, that was wrong.

Her mouth lifted in the corners. She'd given nothing away, only gained something. Some power. Some control. She had exercised a deeply personal right. To choose her first lover. Before one was chosen for her.

Did she regret it?

She pressed her thighs together, the movement causing the apple to wobble, and thought of the gentle caresses, the soft sighs, as natural and calming as the falling night rain.

The sight of her lover, tall, broad-shouldered, filling her vision as he held himself levered above her. The hot, heady smell of his skin. The contrast of her pale hand against the bronze of his hard-muscled arm.

She shivered.

No. She did not regret it.

She looked out over the arena, at the crowds filing into the stalls for a good seat to the spectacle. Above her, a bird cried, the sound haunting, and she shaded her eyes and searched the skies for it. Yearned to leap from the glass peak and fly to join it, leave the crowds and her fate behind her.

As if on cue with her thoughts of fate, one by one the knights arrived. They were a rainbow swirl of blue, green, yellow and red plumes and banners, polished metal shining almost as much at the glass mountain.

They paraded, playing the crowd, racing in a loop down the length of the course and around the mountain. Getting the measure of what they were up against.

She recognized a few of them. Some were her father's own men —men she'd known since they were boys come as knights-in-training—some were in service to other kings, princes and lords. All were here for one thing.

Power.

They intended to use her, to take this opportunity offered by her father and exploit it, and by dint of taking part in this contest at all, they had her unreserved contempt.

They obviously felt the same way about her, as not one so much as glanced her way. She was but a means to an end, and for her father to put her in this position was unsupportable. Incredible.

3

As she thought about what he'd done to her, bands of steel tightened across her chest.

Kayla gasped for air, every gulp like breathing the poisonous smoke of a tanner's fire, burning her throat, all the way down to her lungs.

The trumpet sounded, and Kayla saw her father standing in his box, dressed in rich red robes, his crown in place. He lifted a hand.

Silence fell, rippling out from the crowd until the only sound was the creak of leather saddles and the huff of horse breath.

"Welcome, gentlemen. The rules are simple. You will each have a chance to ride your horse up the glass mountain, and pluck the golden apple from my daughter's lap. Whoever succeeds will have my daughter's hand and become the heir to my kingdom."

The knights let out a cheer—dogs barking as their master threw them a bone. Kayla wondered how happy they'd be to know the bone had been tasted already. Her lips curved. Oh, she did not regret last night for even a moment.

"Is every competitor present?" the herald called out.

There was a murmur of assent, and then a shuffle of horses near the gates.

A late-comer?

Kayla almost deigned not to look. What did she care how many and who? But the murmurs of the crowd piqued her curiosity, and she raised a hand to shield her eyes and saw him.

A knight all in black, on a black horse.

Her heart gave a traitorous lurch at the figure he cut, his mount dancing through the crowd, moving toward her shimmering perch.

He was the first to approach her. Acknowledge her.

And when he was close enough, he raised his visor.

The breath caught in Kayla's throat. Her heart stuttered.

Bright blue eyes looked up at her. No longer warm and laughing as they had been last night, but cold with purpose.

He turned with a salute and rode back to the waiting pack, and she clenched her skirts with white-knuckled fists.

Whatever she had to do, she would make sure he was the one.

"WHAT IN HELL IS THAT THING?" Jasper stood with Rane in the knights' holding pen and eyed the glass monstrosity with dislike. Rane knew it was an unwelcome obstacle to Jasper's plans.

Usually anything that was a problem for Jasper was cause for celebration in Rane's view, but in this instance, Jasper's goal was his own. For the last time, though.

"A glass mountain."

"I can see that, but where'd the king get it?" Jasper's plump face was unusually pale.

"Dark magic," Rane answered shortly. He could feel magic coming off the thing. Crackling the air around it. Snapping at him. And Kayla sat on top of it, her face blank and white. At its mercy.

As she was at yours just last night, his conscience whispered. And did you not take from her her only bargaining chip?

He fisted his reins in the heavy black gloves and his mount moved uneasily beneath him, sensitive to his mood.

Of all the stains on his soul, letting Kayla of Gaynor think she was seducing him while he reeled her in as finely as any master would be the hardest to wash clean.

She'd been determined to give away her virginity last night and oh, she was sweet.

He had no excuse.

He could have walked away, but he did not. Even as she whispered her joy at the taking, moaned his name, knifes of disgust tore through his heart.

Why had he not walked away?

He'd meant only to gain her favor. Become her favorite, even while she thought he was not participating in the contest. So when he did appear, it would seem as if he'd come to save her.

He'd been here days before the others, and he knew full well the task set was impossible. The only way to succeed was with help.

And who could help him more in this than the princess herself?

"Rane? Are you listening?"

5

MICHELLE DIENER

He jerked his head down, saw Jasper's impatience in his stiff bearing. "Yes?"

"You said dark magic. Who would oblige the king so?"

It wasn't impatience making Jasper so tense, Rane realized—it was fear.

He shrugged. What did he care whose power the king made use of for his strange husband-choosing?

"I've heard whispers that a few of the kings in the Middleland have a sorcerer obliging them, these days. Now the King of Gaynor?" Jasper rubbed the side of his face, and Rane noticed his fingers trembled.

"You suspect some plot?" Rane controlled his expression as Jasper flinched at his words. He'd never seen Jasper this rattled.

The sheer size and magnificence of the mountain, the strangeness of it, pointed to someone of immense power. And Jasper was in the business of power. Rane knew Jasper thought he had an edge with a sorcerer for a brother, but if the King of Gaynor had a sorcerer of this caliber on his side, there were few who could stand in his way.

"No. . . No. I wonder who the sorcerer is, that's all."

"The question should rather be, why is the king making the trial so difficult? Why does he want a fighter and a madman for his daughter?"

Jasper's eyes widened. "You think he wants a bodyguard for her?"

Rane had not, but it was a good point. One to ponder. "I thought he might have a further quest in mind. One that would take more than a spoilt prince to accomplish. A quest he could trust only to his future heir."

"With this trial he can sidestep the rules of royal marriage, and find the best man for the job, even if he is a commoner." Jasper nodded his head slowly.

"Only a theory." Rane's eyes swung back to the magic hill, back to the woman in her white gown, her dark hair woven with tiny white flowers and flowing over her shoulders. Hair he'd grabbed in fistfuls, felt like silk between his fingers as he exposed her throat to

6

his mouth. Hair that twined round his arms as he'd taken them both to a better place for a while.

Jasper's gaze turned curious, and Rane regretted his thoughts. Regretted what must have passed across his face.

"Just get me the apple, and you can have your brother back, and all the pleasures that come with marriage to the royal house. Or not." Jasper shrugged. "Walk away from it all if you choose, if the king has a more dangerous job in mind for you than impregnating his daughter. I don't care."

Rane didn't clamp down on his hatred fast enough. Some of it must have flashed across his face for Jasper's eyes to narrow.

"Any hint of a double-cross, Rane, and you'll never see your good-for-nothing brother again." Jasper paused and his face hardened. "Except maybe in little pieces."

CHAPTER 2

With a scream, the horse slid down the mountain on its side, flailing and bucking as it went. Its rider hung on desperately, staying in the saddle until they hit the ground.

The horse rolled, and with a scream of his own, the rider was crushed beneath it.

When the horse scrambled up and ran for the fence, the knight lay still, and there was a moment of silence from the crowd.

Then, as if released from some dark spell, everyone began to shout and move at once. Two men ran to the fallen knight, far more tried to get the horse under control.

Kayla lifted her stricken gaze from the disaster below and looked across at her father. How many more? She wanted to scream the question. How many more must leave maimed or dead?

He stared back, his face impassive, tight with control. He lifted his hand, gave a wave.

On with the contest.

Kayla blinked against the tears that threatened to spill. She was so weary of tears. She sat stiff and unyielding. Refusing to wilt.

She wondered which victim would be next. There were only four left, but when she turned to the holding pen, she saw three of the final number leaving. Deserting the field.

Leaving only the knight in black.

Rane De'Villier.

Secretary and aide to Jasper of Harness. He sat on his horse well, looked comfortable in his armor, but Kayla knew he was a man of poetry and words, not action. He had not been trained in the ways of a knight.

Her heart thundered in her chest. She could not pretend it didn't thrill her that he had come today.

His determination to win her set her senses alight, more brilliant and blinding than the midday sun off the glass mountain.

It made last night real. Perfect. Not a hastily snatched tryst, but true love.

The cold truth was, though, he should not attempt it.

She was glad he wanted to win her, but she did not want it to cost him his life.

He came out of the holding pen, horse prancing, and looked up at the mountain, sizing it up, taking its measure. Steeling himself.

His horse danced under him, eager or nervous.

The noise from the stalls was a dull roar. Like an ocean in full storm.

He raised his hand in salute to the crowd, and urged his mount forward, gathering speed, taking the run faster, straighter, than any knight before him.

His horse's hooves hit the glass with a high pitched 'ting', the sound of the most expensive crystal hit with a silver spoon, and it seemed to gain a grip, as if there were studs on its shoes.

His visor was up, and Kayla could see the intense focus in Rane's eyes, the pure determination.

He was close. Closer than any other had come, perhaps more than halfway up the slope. She looked down at the gleaming apple. Thought back to what it had done to her earlier and braced herself for the pain.

In a single, smooth movement her fingers closed over it, and she threw.

Light arced again from the apple to her palm, a white-hot

connection of agony. As she cried out, Rane raised a black-gloved hand and snatched it from the air.

The light strobed from between his fingers, its connection to her stronger than before, the pain flaring to a peak, then winking out. Replaced by a terrible sense of urgency. But Kayla did not know what she must do to still the thundering of her heart.

As if in some strange dream, where every action is slowed by half, she watched Rane turn the horse, lifting from the saddle as it plunged down the slope.

As they slid away from her, she felt the pull of the apple, like a hard jerk, trying to yank her out of her chair.

She fought it, her lips a white, clenched line of panic, her hands clinging to the chair arms, her feet scrabbling for purchase.

Rane's horse hit the ground, galloping and dancing in terror away from the mountain, pulling her with it, the arc of light stretched to its elastic limit.

The force hauled at her, strong as ten men. Kayla teetered on the edge of the precipice. Her gaze clashed with her black knight's as he turned back to her, apple held high, and then, with a wild cry, she fell.

THERE WAS a thin white chain of light pulling Kayla from her chair. Rane saw too late it was connected to the apple, that it had somehow manacled her hand and dragged her with it as he rode across the field, his prize held up for all to see. To witness.

The mountain throbbed more malevolently than before as she flew over the edge and down.

He urged his horse forward, but it refused to take what it thought was another run at the mountain. It raised its forelegs and tried to dislodge him, and with a curse he leapt from the saddle.

Kayla was sliding down the slope, her skirts fluttering and lifting, her arms spread wide. Her face stricken.

He ran toward her, but she was coming too fast. Her feet hit the ground and she pitched forward, her eyes wide with fear. Her body slammed into the ground with a thud, sliding in the mud churned up by the horses from the spongy, wet earth.

When he reached her, he realized the damned apple was still in his hand, and he dropped it beside her as he knelt.

She opened her eyes, but they were unfocused, her forehead smeared with mud. She struggled to roll onto her side, to curl up in an instinctive movement of self-protection.

Her hands accidentally brushed the apple as she moved, and her body gave a jolt, as if she'd been bitten by a viper.

Her eyes opened again, this time with a snap, their focus clear and sharp. She blinked at the sight of him, then her gaze fell to the apple, resting against the back of her hand.

"It healed me." Her voice was a strange mixture of horror and relief.

Rane looked down at the thing. Thought of how badly Jasper wanted it. How he was willing even to let Soren go in exchange for it, and understanding hit him.

"What did it heal?" He drew off his glove and laid a finger on it. Felt a strange, unpleasant tingle, and lifted his hand.

"My legs, my feet. They were broken." She struggled up, bent a knee and kneaded her slippered foot with a hand. "I hit the ground so hard, I heard the bones snap."

Suddenly, she gasped. "What is happening?"

Rane frowned. There was nothing happening, and that was wrong. The King's men should be here, the princess's ladies-in-waiting. He turned, and saw the crowd standing ten feet away from them.

They were staring in open-mouthed amazement.

Rane stood and held out a hand, helped Kayla to her feet. The front of her gossamer white dress was caked in mud, her body plastered with it.

She barely came to his shoulder.

Standing there, he felt the creeping sense there was something undone. Some task he needed to complete.

"The light," she said.

He looked down at her. "The light?"

"From the apple. It's keeping the crowd back."

Rane focused on the apple, still lying in the mud at their feet. It glowed like a fire, its light difficult to see in the bright sunshine, but there all the same, encasing them in its golden rays.

Kayla shivered, then clutched him as the day seemed to dim and flicker, as if the sun were a candle flame, blowing in the wind.

"The light's gone now," she said.

Rane looked up and saw what had replaced it was much, much worse.

CHAPTER 3

a man strode onto the field, pushing aside anyone in his way, using his staff to clear his path, sending men and women tumbling.

Kayla's grip on Rane's arm tightened.

The man stopped just short of them, and Kayla saw he was incredibly handsome. His hair was almost white blond, his eyes shockingly dark.

"What is this?" He spoke as if he had a right to ask, as if he'd ordered them to do something else, and they had disobeyed him.

Kayla felt a flare of anger at his tone, and from the way Rane stiffened under her fingers, he did, too. But beneath her sense of outrage, was another, hovering sense that this man did have a right.

She saw his eyes flick over both of them, as if searching for something, and then focus on the ground. On the apple.

He took a step closer, to pick it up, and Rane stepped to block him. His movement spoke of suppressed violence. Of perfect control.

It occurred to her that he did not seem very like a secretary and a poet any more.

"You will regret standing in my way." The stranger's eyes narrowed.

Rane bent and picked up the apple with his other, gloved hand.

"I took this apple from the princess of Gaynor in a test of skill." Rane lifted the apple up and looked at it curiously. "It belongs to me."

Kayla gaped at him. Of all the things she'd expected him to say, this was not it. What did either of them care for the odious apple? He had fought to win *her*, surely? The apple was irrelevant.

"Something isn't right." The stranger was staring at them both. His black cloak rippled about him, and Kayla felt the icy hand of fear brush the back of her neck. The breeze had died half an hour ago. The mid-morning was airless and there was no playful wind to make his cloak dance.

He drew both hands up, his staff raised, and the day darkened again, just as it had when he'd arrived.

"Halt."

Her father's voice carried enough weight, enough power, to make even the stranger freeze.

"Step back, Eric the Bold."

At the mention of the stranger's name, there was a gasp from the crowd, and as a single body, they backed away from him. Some ran.

"King Haren. What mischief have you wrought?" Eric lowered his arms, and the daylight seeped back into the sky. "What have you done to my golden apple?"

"The question is what have you done, Eric?" Her father looked gaunt. Years older than he'd been just yesterday. "It was a simple prize, you said. The initial lure, a foretaste of what could be gained. They would know even if I found a way to weasel out of my promises, it was a solid reason to enter the contest."

Eric's lips thinned. "I hold the power here, Haren. I told you what I wished to tell you. You do not question *me*."

"Lure?" Kayla heard the chill of a midwinter wind in Rane's voice. "What do you mean, lure?"

Was it her imagination, or were his words weary and bitter. Disenchanted.

Eric the Bold turned back to them. She noticed his hand gripped the top of his staff, his knuckles showing white.

"You cheated," he said, his lips drawn back over his teeth like a snarling dog. "You must have cheated."

Rane looked at her. The first time since he'd stepped forward to claim the apple. There was deep regret in his eyes, and she suddenly felt cold little shivers of fear, of panic, running down her spine.

"There was no other way to win. The task was impossible." He kept his eyes on her, but she could not hold his gaze.

"I expected the winner to cheat. To be inventive. But you ruined it, somehow. What did you do?" Without warning, Eric lifted his staff and pressed the end to Rane's chest. "What did you do?" He tapped the staff against Rane with every word.

Kayla looked from her father, stark-faced, a stranger to her now, at the powerful stranger he'd called Eric the Bold, and at the darkest stranger of them all, Rane De'Villier.

She swallowed, tried to focus through the ringing in her ears, the heavy weight of betrayal pressing on her chest. What a fool she had been. What a fool.

She stepped forward, waited for every eye to be on her. Drew herself tall.

"He used *me*."

RANE REALIZED the dark wizard called Eric the Bold was still pointing his staff at him, and with a sharp movement of his arm he flicked it away.

He knew who Eric was, no one who'd ever lived in Jasper's stronghold could escape that name. But he'd always imagined he'd look like Jasper's brother, Nuen. Thin, crabbed and sly.

That he stood as high as Rane himself, was as broad in the shoulders and well-muscled, should have been in his favor. But his eyes took away any advantage of his physique. They were pure evil. Power concentrated to a point of no return.

Rane reluctantly looked away from him to Kayla, felt guilt tighten his chest.

She stood with her hands crossed under her breasts, and he realized she had forgotten she was covered in mud. Her posture regal, every line in her body screamed contempt and disdain for all of them.

"As the princess says, I gained my aid from her."

Eric's attention fixed on Kayla. "Princess?"

"She was ripped from her chair and slid down your mountain." The King spoke in tones so measured and cold, Rane glanced at him, waiting for him to lose hold of his control. "You guaranteed she would not be hurt. I have to say I'm amazed to see her standing." His voice broke on the last word.

Kayla's gaze snapped to him, a frown on her face.

"She broke her feet and legs when she landed." Rane watched Eric with hooded eyes. If the wizard was responsible for Kayla's fall from the mountain, the king would have to stand in line.

"The apple pulled me off the mountain, and the apple healed me." Kayla finally glanced toward him, but her eyes were on the apple in his hand, not his face.

Eric turned white, his skin almost the same shade as his hair. "If the apple pulled you off, it means you touched it . . ." He lifted his hand, as if to strike her.

Rane moved his ungloved hand to his sword.

"A sword won't stop me." Eric focused on Rane and suddenly Rane's feet were rooted to the spot. He could not move. Could do nothing. He was a statue—

With a jerk, he was released. Ridiculously, he had to gulp for air.

"You've ruined everything." Eric jabbed a finger at Rane, and when he lowered it to stroke his staff there was a tremble in his hand. He flicked a glance at Kayla, and Rane wanted to put himself in front of her, smash in the sorcerer's teeth. There was something of the swamp in Eric's eye.

Rane saw the sorcerer's jaw work. Eric was grinding his teeth. "There is nothing for it. The princess will have to go with you."

"No." The King of Gaynor's cry was tormented. "She was to stay out of this."

"She interfered. You interfered, too, didn't you, old man?" Eric still hadn't unclamped his jaw, and he spoke through gritted teeth. "You thought changing the rules, making the contest for her hand in marriage would change things. You were right. They are changed." His fingers clenched around the staff. "For both of us, they are changed for the worse."

Rane looked between the two men. The conversation did not bode well for a quick hand-over of the apple to Jasper in exchange for Soren, and then he'd be on his way.

He was going to regret this question. "Go where?"

CHAPTER 4

They assembled in her father's chamber, Kayla later than the others, because she'd had to wash the mud off and change.

They didn't sit in the comfortable chairs beside the fire, but at what she'd always thought of as the Council of War table.

And the phrase was more than apt now.

Kayla looked at the golden apple, placed before Rane, and again felt the whisper of disquiet, a panicked feeling that she'd forgotten something, had failed to complete what was required of her.

She noticed Rane's gaze was focused on it as well, and then suddenly, she was ensnared by the intense blue of his eyes. Before she wrenched away, she thought the terrible, heart-pounding sense of a task left unfinished was something they shared.

"The apple holds you." Eric the Bold watched her from across the table, and Kayla saw the anger rise like a riptide across his features as he spoke.

"Just tell us what spell you imbued in my damn apple, and let's be done with it." Rane's voice was cold, hard. Completely emotionless.

She really had not known him. How could she, in three days? And yet she'd thought she did.

"At the moment you feel uncomfortable. Ill at ease. By tomorrow, you will be agitated. You will be compelled to undertake a task for me." Eric leaned back in his chair and steepled his fingers together. The action was measured, his fingers still, but Kayla had the sense he was exercising huge control to keep them from shaking with rage.

"Because of your interference," he dipped his head in her direction, "the spell I placed on the apple has enchanted you both. The task of taking the apple off the mountain was only accomplished because you worked together. You will both have to go." He sucked in a deep breath, and suddenly slammed clenched fists on the table. Ground them into the smooth wood.

Rane leaned forward, the movement easy. "And if we don't?"

"You will go mad." A thread of spiteful malice ran through the frustration in Eric's voice.

Kayla watched him, at the rage thrumming through him at having his plans foiled, and wondered what plan he'd had in mind for her before she interfered.

A long, slow shiver ran down her spine.

It gave her a sense of dark satisfaction that she had to go, then, despite the company she would have to keep.

"And when we have undertaken the task?" Kayla mirrored Eric, placing fisted hands on the table.

"When you have found the item I need and given it to me, I'll end the enchantment." Eric paused, and then looked sidelong at her father, sitting like stone throughout the conversation, eyes closed. "And you are all free to do as you please."

"What is this item, and why don't you get it yourself?" Rane's voice was quiet.

"It's a jewel. Held by a witch."

Kayla stared at him. "You want us to ask her for it?"

Rane gave a dry laugh. "If it were that easy, he'd have done it himself. Instead he's staged this elaborate charade to find someone with the guts and skill to get things that are impossible to get, and enchanted his golden apple to make sure they undertake his . . .

task. You can be sure the only way to get this jewel will be to steal it."

Eric clapped his hands, the sound jerking her father from his thoughts. "Bravo. I am, as it happens, too powerful. Ylana will sense me long before I reach her door. I need someone with no magical power. Someone who would be able to get my jewel the hard way."

The hard way.

There was an ominous ring to the expression.

Rane stared down at the apple again. Kayla thought he sagged for a moment, just one blink of the eye, then straightened again. All hard eyes and sneering mouth.

"Where does this witch live?"

"The Great Forest." Eric spoke quietly, this time. As well he should.

Kayla found herself half-standing before she realized she'd left her chair. Rane was already up and her father had drawn a dagger, pointing it at Eric's throat. If the king had not dismissed the guards from the room, Eric would have had two swords at his throat, as well.

"You would send my daughter into the *Great Forest?*" The dagger shook along with her father's arm.

"I don't want her to go." Eric ignored the knife, his focus on her father's face. "There is no choice. Do you want her a gibbering madwoman? Unless she goes, that is what she will become."

"Because of you! Because you enchanted that apple." With a cry, her father raised the dagger and plunged it into the table.

For a moment, they all watched it quiver like a live thing in the wood.

"You know our chances in the Great Forest." Rane's words were bitter.

"I would rather the witch lived anywhere else. Anywhere but that hell-begotten place." Eric lifted his hands and ran them through his hair. "I cannot set foot there, myself. I'm not welcome."

"Then we have no choice." Rane stepped away from the table. Looked across at her. "Let's be going. I have a pressing need for this apple. The sooner I'm clear of any enchantments, the better." He lifted the apple with a bare hand, not flinching, and then locked gazes with Eric. "Do I have your word when you have the jewel, the enchantment will end?"

Eric brushed his hand over his staff, and Kayla thought suddenly how ridiculous the gesture was. It was affected, as if he were fifty years older than he was.

"You have my word."

Rane made no reply to that. He stood, quite still, his lean, muscled frame taking up more room than it should. He turned back to her.

"Be ready to leave in half an hour. Wear men's clothing so you don't slow us down." He made for the door, and Kayla gaped at his back, too stunned to move.

Her father took a step toward him, his gait unsteady. "Who do you think you are, to talk to my daughter that way?"

Rane put his hand on the door knob, looked over his shoulder and gave a grim smile. "Sir, by your own announcement, I am her betrothed."

HER BETROTHED.

This morning, it would have been her dream come true. Now it was a nightmare that had no end in sight.

He was serious about leaving immediately, and she wondered why he needed the apple so badly. She frowned. Payment for a gaming debt, perhaps? Or he had a buyer for it.

Or perhaps, like her, the terrible sense of panic at not being underway drove him.

She reached back to loosen the ties on her gown. Gertie had unknotted them for her before going off in search of men's clothing, muttering under her breath as she went. Kayla eased loose the top two eyelets and stilled.

Turned to the door.

Her father stood there, and pain stabbed her straight through the heart.

He fidgeted like a stranger. Like a man who was unsure of his welcome.

"Yes?" She hated her tone. Hated the sharp edge to it. She was incapable of stopping herself. Hurt and betrayal had honed her voice fine as a razor's tip.

"I don't want you to go alone with De'Villier." He finally took a step into the room. "Especially into the Great Forest."

That made two of them. She didn't want to be alone with De'Villier either. And the Forest was the dream-scape of her nightmares. "You've made him my betrothed, Father. There is little enough between marriage and betrothal as it is. And the circumstances—"

"To hell with the circumstances!"

She jumped at his shout. Had to exert incredible control to keep herself steady.

"What would you have me do? Take Gertie? Take a knight? A cook? A stablehand?" She tossed her head. "Take a crowd into the Forest, when we need to be thieves in the night? When the price of failure is my descent into madness?" She fisted her hands. She could feel the tug of desperation, the enchantment, growing stronger. Could well imagine what would happen to her if she failed to go, and go quickly. "De'Villier may be a liar and a user, but he seems to know what he's doing."

"You always were headstrong." Her father rubbed his hands over his face. "I encouraged it, I know. Thought it delightful. Loved the way you sent every suitor on his way. If your mother were alive, she'd no doubt have reined you in more."

"That would have suited you better, if I'd been more docile. When you tried to sell me off for the price of a golden apple."

"Not just a golden apple. The kingdom, too." His correction was soft. "Don't forget, De'Villier becomes the next king."

"No." She pointed a finger. "Don't *you* forget." She drew in a deep breath. Let it out in an explosive rush. "Why? Why did you do it?"

"Do you think I had a choice?" His words came out in a hiss of frustration. "Eric made it very clear. Find him a knight up to the job he needed, or ..."

"Or?"

He shook his head. Walked to the door. "What does it matter, now?" He looked over his shoulder, and she thought she saw a glimmer of moisture in his eye. "Take care, Kayla. The Forest ... not many come out of it the same. If they come out at all. Especially these days." The door closed behind him with a click.

She stood, lost in thought, her hands plucking and pulling her laces, until her gown fell to her feet. Today changed the reality of the last month. Changed the way she looked at things.

Nothing was as it seemed.

The door to her chamber swung open, and she turned in relief, expecting Gertie.

Rane De'Villier stood in the doorway. He had changed from his knight's armour, and wore trousers as dark brown as his hair, a loose, white shirt over it.

He looked like an adventurer.

"I said thirty minutes." He looked at her for a long beat, and it took her a moment to remember she was standing half-naked in the center of her room. Looking at him had chased all thoughts from her mind.

Her body was remembering him, where her heart and mind would forget.

She held his gaze, forcing all feelings of vulnerability away. "You also said I must dress as a man, and as it happens, trousers and shirts are not a staple of my wardrobe. I'm waiting for my maid to find me some."

She turned her back on him, she could not bear him staring at her that way any longer. As if she were merely an inconvenience.

"Your highness?" Gertie stood behind Rane, her voice tentative. "I have found some clothes I think will fit."

Kayla looked over her shoulder, glared at Rane. "Bring them here, please, Gertie."

Gertie squeezed passed Rane's imposing presence, and came to stand next to Kayla. She wavered, uncertain, the clothes in her hand. Looked back at Rane, looming at the entrance.

Kayla kept all irritation from her face, and raised an eyebrow.

He raised his own. "I will carry you out as you are if you do not dress right now. It is already past midday."

She ground her teeth and took the clothes, yanking on trousers of thick, dark blue cotton. The shirt was much like her newly betrothed was wearing, and she loved the cool feel of it.

"I have three extra shirts and one extra pair of trousers, your highness." Gertie packed them neatly in her cloth bag. "The kitchen is loading the horses' saddlebags with supplies."

Kayla looked up from pulling on her riding boots. "Thank you." She stood, and took a few steps in her new attire. It felt good.

She smiled as sweetly as she was able to manage at Rane. "Ready to go."

CHAPTER 5

*P*erhaps it would have been easier if he hadn't slept with her. But Rane doubted it.

Seeing Kayla of Gaynor in broad daylight in next to nothing had been bad for his heart. And when she'd turned her back—every inch the cool, haughty princess—he'd had the pleasure of a rear view.

The same one he was looking at right now, this time covered in the taut material of the trousers her disapproving maid had found for her. The sight was only marginally less enticing than it had been earlier.

She swung angrily down the passageway of her family's small, quaint castle, as chilly and stiff as she'd been warm and pliant last night.

She was all smooth curves and lean muscle. A fit, athletic woman. That was how he'd first hooked her. He'd seen her riding. Knew he could use it to come to her attention.

He'd deliberately faked a riding accident, miles from the castle.

She'd been quite alone. He'd seen how she rode out by herself, hard and fast, for hours on end. It had been a gift for a man bent on seduction and betrayal.

He'd accomplished both quite nicely.

Something akin to despair gripped him.

Until this morning, he'd been able to look himself in the mirror with respect. He'd lost that today.

Once Rane handed the apple to Jasper and Soren was free, his brother was on his own. No more rescues. If he wanted to continue his mindless campaign against Jasper, Soren would have to accept the consequences.

Rane was going to make that very, very clear.

"I thought we were in a hurry?"

Rane snapped back to the present, and saw Kayla waiting for him at the head of the stairs. She bristled with hostility and hurt. But there was something more in her eyes. The same rising urgency to be off that was affecting him.

He could do nothing about either.

"We are." Rane lengthened his stride. "I want to make some progress before nightfall."

"Something is driving you besides this enchantment. What is so pressing, De'Villier? Why the rush?" She watched him warily, her arms crossed over her chest. So different to her usual manner.

His was the final betrayal, he realized. Her father's behavior had puzzled and wounded her, she hadn't been able to make sense of it. But he'd come along, and for a few days, she'd trusted him. What he'd done to her had closed the door on her open nature and thrown the bolt.

He wondered what she would do if he told her his brother was being beaten and tortured every day he delayed handing that apple over. He doubted she'd believe him. Or care.

Because he'd changed her future, upended her world in exchange for Soren's freedom.

"My business." He stepped around her and ran lightly down the worn stone steps. "And it won't wait."

"De'Villier." Eric the Bold was waiting for him as he stepped into the bright sunlight of the rear courtyard.

After the cool, dim light of the castle, he was forced to shield his eyes. Forced to stop a moment.

He sensed Kayla behind him, just within the castle doors. She

26

had stopped at the sight of Eric, had held back, withdrawing to the deep shadows.

Rane turned to the sorcerer and waited.

"I would suggest you leave my apple here for safekeeping." Eric's hand was extended.

Rane waited another beat. Waited to see if he felt compelled to hand it over.

He did not.

Interesting.

"Your apple, sorcerer?" He forced his face into a parody of confusion.

"Slip of the tongue. I meant your apple, of course. It's been mine so long, you'll forgive my little mistake." Eric flicked his hands as if ridding himself of a pesky fly.

"I believe in safeguarding what is mine." Rane did not move.

"I'm glad we're in agreement. I would not want Ylana to get her hands on that apple." Again, Eric extended his hand.

"I am quite capable of safeguarding my own treasures." Rane turned and walked toward the horses. The king stood to one side of them, attended by his courtiers—a nervous huddle of brightly colored fish, their mouths opening and closing in shock at the speed and strangeness of events.

Behind him, there was dead silence. Then the door creaked, and he heard Kayla step out.

He turned, and saw Eric staring at her with the intensity of a snake at a mouse. She looked spectacular in her men's clothing. But the expression on the sorcerer's face was more than just lascivious. It was possessive.

Rane's heart gave a long, hard beat, an emotion he could not name rearing in his chest. He did not take his eyes from her as she came to him.

"Don't turn your back on that sorcerer again," she murmured when she reached him. Her face was neutral, but her eyes were deep pools of fear.

Rane had to swallow before he could reply. "Had a little difficulty accepting my rejection of his offer, did he?" He laced his fingers and offered her a leg up he knew she didn't need.

She slipped a booted foot into the cradle of his hands. "I'm quite sure if he hadn't needed you to get his jewel, he'd have killed you."

THEY WERE WELL-MATCHED RIDERS.

He was not the inept secretary who couldn't keep a seat on a horse. More like the knight who'd managed the impossible and ridden a thundering charger up a glass mountain.

Funny, but she had a deep sense he was neither extreme. Or only the hard-bitten knight when he was forced to be.

But what was forcing him, now?

She was irritated she felt the need to get a sense of him at all. He wasn't worth her time. Just a sideways glance at him as he rode alongside her was enough to remind her of how he took her, used her, made a lie of what she'd thought they'd had.

She caught his eye, and her feelings must have been plain on her face, because he gave a slight grimace and urged his horse ahead.

She set her teeth, and concentrated on ignoring his back.

They were making good time through the open fields. The occasional farmer raised a hand to them as they thundered passed, but only Kayla waved back.

Fragrant mid-summer grass scented the hot afternoon air, and the corn rippled and swayed lazily in a gentle breeze. Gaynor was not called the gem of the Middleland for nothing. It glowed green as an emerald.

There would be a record harvest this year.

It occurred to Kayla the terrible sense of panic, of desperation to do what needed to be done, had begun to ease. She felt it lift perceptibly, an indescribable relief.

They must be getting closer to their goal.

They were climbing all the time, though the gradient was barely noticeable. The road skirted most of the villages, giving them a clear run north, and if she narrowed her eyes, she could see the hills in the distance.

The first touch of cool air flowed down to them from the escarpment, carrying the tang of pine and dark earth. She filled her lungs, lifted her hair off her neck and the breeze caught it and held it off her skin with soothing fingers.

The Great Forest stretched along Gaynor's north boundary, a natural fence, and spilled deep into Therston. Kayla recalled Jasper of Harness was from Therston—Rane must be, too. They may well be journeying near De'Villier's home.

"Did Eric tell you where this witch is to be found?"

His head came up, as if she'd pulled him from his own reverie, and he eased his horse back. Gave a short nod. "He did, while you were getting ready for the journey. The heart of the Forest."

"Would that put her in Therston?"

Rane shook his head. "Probably the southern tip of Klevan. Not that there will be any real way to tell."

He was right. The forest was so dense, the kingdom boundaries were no more than lines on a map. Unchanged for centuries.

She glanced at the sun, sinking west to the left of them. "We should reach the forest by nightfall." She was making conversation, unwilling to go back to the stony silence of before.

The sound of the horses' hooves on the hard-packed soil of the road and her own breathing were suddenly too lonely.

"Have you ever been in the Great Forest?" Something in his question made her wary.

"With my father. Three years ago." She didn't elaborate, or tell him they had gone no further than ten trees deep.

"Things are very different there, these days." He held her gaze, and she looked uncomfortably away. Her father had said the same thing.

"We'll stop at the edge tonight. Continue our journey in daylight."

She lifted a hand from the reins and brushed a lock of hair out of her eyes. "Too hard-going in the dark?"

He hunched his shoulders, tipping his weight forward on his horse and urging it faster. "Too dangerous."

CHAPTER 6

*T*he urgency, the terrible, throat-clawing panic that had gripped him in Gaynor Castle had lifted as they'd reached the foot of the escarpment, leaving him light. Leaving him determined not to have it return.

But as soon as they stopped for the night it crept back, insidious as fog. Rane lifted his head and took in the first line of trees against a dusk-darkened sky. He wished it was safe to continue.

He knew it was not.

The princess was just within the trees, he could hear her muttering as she tripped over the branches she was supposed to be gathering. She'd taken to the task of finding wood far more readily than he'd thought. In fact, she'd taken this whole trip in her stride. He'd expected more saddlebags, a request for a servant, and far more sulking.

There'd been none of that.

The small pile of wood he was coaxing into a blaze smouldered sullenly and then winked out in a choking billow of smoke. The wood was wet.

He'd told her he'd get the fire going, but mere flint stones were not going to give them a fire tonight.

And they needed one.

Rane had not grown up in Therston, on the western edge of this same forest, without knowing at least that much. As it was, he knew a lot more.

He heard Kayla wander a little further into the trees than he'd like, but he took advantage of the opportunity. He slipped his hand into the pouch at his belt and took out a thin black stick, only slightly longer than his middle finger. It tapered to a point at one end. He turned it in his hand and touched it to the wood.

A flame leapt high, the suddenness of the heat causing a pop and crack as the wet wood was engulfed in fire.

"That looks good." Kayla stepped out from the trees, her arms loaded with branches. The light flickered wildly over her face and seemed to lean toward her. She looked fey and dangerous. "I thought it would take you longer with that wet wood."

Without any sudden moves, although his heart had lurched at her appearance, Rane calmly slid the stick back into his pouch and picked up his flint stones. Knocked them together so a little spark flew. "Practice," he said.

There was silence, and he thought for a moment she was going to challenge him. Call him a liar.

Instead she dropped the branches she'd collected. "I went deeper under the trees and found some drier wood."

"Good." He stood, going to the saddlebags. "Let's see what the kitchens of Gaynor castle have given us."

She said nothing, easing herself down onto one of the rocks near the fire. She looked tired. Drained. But he knew it wasn't the ride. She could probably ride double the distance they had done today with ease.

"What's wrong?" He regretted the question as soon as it left his lips.

She raised her eyes, regarded him a long moment. Shook her head and swung back to the fire.

He thought there might have been the sparkle of a tear on her cheek, and he turned quickly to the saddle bags and their dinner.

It seemed his brother wasn't the only idiot in his family.

THE BITE of panic was back in Kayla's chest, squeezing her with relentless jaws, forcing her from sleep.

Breathing hard, she came up off the thick pallet, and locked eyes with Rane De'Villier. He was sitting near the fire, and she had the feeling he'd been there a while, watching her.

He said nothing, the fire glowing between them, but along with the regret in his eyes there was understanding. He wished he could leave now, like her. Run into the forest just to ease the terrible sensation.

They shared the torment of the golden apple the same way prisoners share the privations of the cell, the indignities of confinement.

They knew something about each other no one else could know.

Of course, he knew more than one thing about her no one else did. She savored her bitterness a moment, then let it go. He had betrayed her trust, but she had given herself freely to him, with no promises between them.

"Let's break camp." Her voice seemed over-loud in the still of deep night.

"If we get lost, we'll go completely mad. And in the dark, with no sun to guide us, we'll get lost." He spoke calmly, without inflection. If she hadn't seen the look in his eyes she might have been fooled into thinking he had shaken the enchantment loose. "Besides, this . . . feeling . . . it's better than running into—"

He broke off suddenly, turned back to the forest, and for a moment she thought it was an excuse to stop talking, to shield her from what he thought they might encounter. As if she didn't know. Or thought she did.

Then she heard it.

The crack of a twig. Crushed under a heavy foot.

Rane rose slowly, hand extended. The light caught his arm, and she saw he was holding a long-bladed, gleaming knife. But its gleam was not from a reflection of the fire. It seemed to have an inner light. It shimmered blue.

He looked over his shoulder at her and lifted a finger to his lips. Made a motion with his hand indicating she should crouch down.

She was suddenly very glad De'Villier was as large and as dangerous as he was. He looked formidable.

She stepped away from the ring of firelight and sank down on her haunches. Behind her, the horses nickered nervously.

She had not brought a single weapon. It hadn't even crossed her mind.

She'd been thinking like a princess, not a thief.

Now her hands felt empty. She clenched them, and searched the ground, straining her eyes in the poor light. There was a branch lying within reach, and she leaned forward and grabbed it. The solid weight of it comforted her.

She looked up at Rane, and blinked in surprise. He was gone.

She held herself still, straining to hear him, but the only sounds were her own breathing and the crackle of the fire.

She waited, crouching until her thighs quivered with the effort and her eyes watered as she searched the darkness for even the smallest movement.

She felt strangely disoriented, as if she'd been spun around and had to cling to the earth to stop herself falling over. She rested her head on her knees and closed her eyes. Tried to see if her ears were the sharper for it.

She could smell the sweet, green smoke of the fire, the strong perfume of dried pine needles, the musty, sharp tang of the stick in her hand.

There was a crash, deep within the trees—the sound of someone falling into a bush or from a high branch to a lower one.

She rose, the muscles in her legs shrieking. She held the stick double-handed, at shoulder height, and was surprised to realize she was shaking. She could not stay here and wait.

She was still in her stocking feet, and she moved to her pallet to pull on her boots before moving into the forest.

When she reached the trees, she hesitated, trying to remember the direction the sound had come from. A voice, just a snatch of a word, drifted to her from the right, and she started toward it.

The first two steps she took sounded like the footsteps of a giant to her. Twigs and dead leaves snapped and crunched beneath her boots, and she stilled. How had De'Villier moved so quietly?

She tried again, going on tip toes, grateful when a small breeze blew up, stirring the debris of the forest floor and masking her steps with a skitter and rustle of sound.

"Where is it?"

The question was so clear, so close, Kayla threw herself against a tree trunk and raised the stick, her gaze swinging wildly from side to side.

"I'm not going to ask again." It was coming from right in front of her.

There was a thump, and she stepped very cautiously forward, aligning herself with another tree, hiding deep within its shadow, adjusting and re-adjusting her grip on the stick.

There was a small clearing before her, illuminated by a man holding a torch in one hand, and Rane De'Villier's neck with the other. A second man stood to one side, the reason why Rane had not escaped. He held a double-sided axe loosely in both hands. The two men had their backs to her, but she could see De'Villier's face in the torchlight. It betrayed no hint of fear, although a thin trickle of blood ran from a cut on Rane's cheek down the side of his face.

"I don't have it yet. Djan, why would I lie?" Rane spoke levelly, calmly. Kayla blinked. It sounded as if he knew the man holding him.

"Don't know. Why would you lie?"

De'Villier sighed, exasperated. "I wouldn't. We're dealing with Eric the Bold. Of course he's trying to worm out of giving me the apple. I won't own it free and clear until I get him what he wants." He lifted his hands in appeal. "Haven't we all heard from Nuen countless times what a twisted bastard Eric is? Why would this be simple, with him involved?"

The man he'd called Djan grunted, and Kayla thought his fingers relaxed their hold a little. She took a step back, to draw deeper into the shadows, and stepped on a dead branch. It rolled under her foot, and she screamed as she fell backwards. The stick she'd held in her hand flew through the air and landed against a tree trunk, with a crack of wood on wood.

There was silence. It rippled out, tense and wary. Kayla lay on the ground, not daring to breathe.

Djan turned toward her, lifting the torch up, his hand falling away from Rane. His face was stone hard and just as cold. He took a step forward. At any moment, the light from the torch would give her away.

Rane gave a shout and Djan spun back to him.

Rane was thrashing against the bush as if attacked by an invisible enemy, and at last Kayla understood. She took the time he was gifting her and rolled toward the nearest tree. Came up in a crouch against it. She looked back at Rane, and as she watched, he vanished into thin air.

"What?" Djan roared, and his companion swung his axe at the bush, scything it like a stand of wheat.

Kayla inched around the tree to the side facing away from the clearing, and began to move away, step by careful step. She reached the next tree, and pressed up against its trunk, listening to see which way Djan and his friend were moving.

Faster than a snake strike, a hand came from behind her and clamped her mouth. She felt her heart stutter, stop, and then race off. Her cry of fear was muffled as the hand clenched tighter.

"It's me."

She realized it was Rane the same instant he spoke. His scent enveloped her, surrounding her as surely as his body did. She went limp, leaning into him, her legs still shaking with shock.

"We need to go back to camp and get our bags. Djan will head there as soon as they go round in circles a time or two." He spoke quietly, directly into her ear.

She nodded into his hand, her lips brushing against his palm, and he released her as if they burned his skin. He stepped around her, and after a moment of hesitation his hand came back to grab hers.

She let him lead the way. She had lost her bearings, her body flinching at every noise from the bush, her mind whirling with questions.

Their camp-fire glowed just ahead, closer than she'd thought, but Rane made them stand still and watch for a long minute before he let them approach.

"We'll have to leave the horses. We can't take them into the forest anyway. Your father can get them back from Jasper when this is over."

"Those were Jasper's men?" She stopped, her mouth falling open with shock.

Rane threw her pack at her, and she caught it absently, and almost toppled as the weight of it jerked her down.

Rane hefted the saddlebags and swung them over his shoulder. "Who did you think I was getting the apple for? Myself?"

"I didn't know—"

"There's plenty you don't know. But now's not the time to discuss it."

He was loaded down, with his own bag and the saddlebags from both horses, and she stepped forward and tugged his bag from his hand.

He let it go. "Don't lose that or let it get into Djan's hands."

"Why not?" She watched him kick dirt on the fire.

"Because the apple's in there."

"Why does this apple mean so much to you?" She stood, legs braced, shoulders balanced by the weight of the two packs, and tried to see his face as the firelight spluttered and was extinguished with a final kick of sand.

His eyes locked with hers a second before they were plunged into darkness. "It's the only thing standing between my brother and a painful death."

CHAPTER 7

They were as good as goats tied to the stake.

Rane didn't know much about this part of the forest, but if it was anything like the western side where he came from, something was watching them right now.

A cry sounded behind them to their right, and he pulled Kayla to him, waited a beat—Djan, he decided with relief.

But they needed to stop. It would be unwise to go deeper, and they couldn't go back.

"We'll wait out the night here," he told her, quiet as the whisper of leaves above them.

He felt her sag with relief in his arms, like the soft surrender of a lover. There was a muffled thud as she dropped their bags on the ground.

They settled back against a trunk, Kayla rubbing aching shoulders, hunching to ease her back after carrying the heavy packs. Rane sat tense, his every sense alert.

When he'd seen Djan, he'd made himself visible, approached him, thinking Jasper had sent him to talk. He hadn't realized Holt was there too, that talking was the last thing on either of their minds.

He touched the empty knife sheath at his belt with regret and looked around for a makeshift weapon. When Djan and Holt had jumped him he'd thrown it behind him. He'd seen Holt use that axe before, and he accepted defeat—but if he'd held onto his knife they would have taken it, no matter that it would look worthless to them, and chances were he'd never have gotten it back. With it lying on the forest floor there was a chance he would.

It was a very special knife. One he'd risked his life to obtain. At first light he'd try to find it. If he was still breathing.

"Don't disappear on me again." Kayla's lips almost brushed his ear.

He flinched. "Why do you say that?"

"You look like you did at the fire. The first time you disappeared. As if you're waiting for danger."

He decided not to deny it. "I might have to."

She shivered. "I'd rather come with you. I don't like waiting and not knowing . . ."

He didn't answer.

"Please."

"I won't leave you alone. I promise."

She nodded. He felt the up-down brush of her hair against his shoulder. Breathed the fragrant heat of her. Tensed a little more.

There was a crash and a shout, alarmingly close, and Kayla clutched his arm. The whole day she'd matched his pace, matched his coolness, matched him at every level. He knew it must cost her to show fear now.

Djan could shout and blunder through the forest all he liked, Rane would not hand over the apple unless he was standing next to Soren when he did it. He would not render his betrayal, all he'd done to get the apple, meaningless.

Rane smiled, a bitter twist of his lips. With the history between Jasper and Soren, there was no way Jasper would give up his brother unless he had no choice. As it was, he must feel an acid burn in his gut at having to release him. If he could get the apple without letting him go, he would.

"Jasper really wants that apple." Kayla's whisper was so close to what he was thinking, he started.

"Yes."

"What will they do when they don't find us?"

"Wait until morning. Try to track us in the light." The tension within him coiled tighter as the hunt moved closer. As Holt's axe swung at bushes and undergrowth, he thought of the whistle and snick of the blade as it brushed his coat earlier when he'd disappeared and Holt had struck out. He fought back a shiver.

He pressed his hands against the ground, as if he could somehow feel the vibrations of Djan and Holt's footsteps, but instead felt a tingle at the back of his neck. The shivery feel of magic, skittering like a spider down his spine.

He froze—rigid—sensed the purple-green energy testing the air, like a thousand dark tongues. He shook off his paralysis, rose in a crouch, and pressed an urgent finger against Kayla's mouth, then pushed her behind him. She did not question him, doing as he wanted without a sound. He felt the quick, frightened rise and fall of her chest against his back.

There was no noise other than the crash and shout of Djan and Holt looking for them, the forest had gone dead still. Like him it seemed to know the nature of the beast.

Wild magic.

SOMETHING WAS MAKING HER ILL. A creeping sense of nausea rose in her throat, and Kayla closed her eyes. Her skin turned cold and clammy and there was a roar in her ears.

She lifted a suddenly trembling hand to her upper lip and wiped away a line of perspiration.

She wanted to speak, to ask Rane what it was they hid from, but she had seen the flash in his eyes as he'd lifted his finger to her lips, and it kept her mouth closed.

He'd been afraid. The first time she'd ever seen that look in his eyes. Climbing the sheer castle wall to her bedroom, racing a charger up a glass mountain to her, even facing down Eric the Bold had not done this to his composure.

She opened her eyes. His back was rigid, as if he were facing off against some invisible monster, his arms clenched so hard she could see the muscles through his shirt and coat, could see the tendons of his neck as they strained in some unseen fight.

She knew she was shivering, but was past caring, past worrying whether he thought her tough and cool-headed. She was too close to vomiting.

She felt a sudden, strange sense of weightlessness, had to close her eyes against the dizziness. She lowered herself down, but instead of the prickle of pine needles and soft sponginess of the forest floor, she felt as if she was floating on air.

Bile rose in her throat and she gasped and curled in on herself, squeezed her eyes closed.

When she was a child, she had gone often to the lake with her mother and thrown herself off the bank into the deep water, somersaulting as she leapt. She felt that same sensation now, but slower, more deliberate, and thought with an uneasy jolt that she must have a fever.

Then the ground was beneath her, as if a soft cloud had been pulled from under her, the pine needles sticking to her palms, digging into them with tiny, sharp pricks.

She'd had no sense of Rane at all for the last few minutes, but she felt him now, turning toward her in the darkness. His wonderfully warm hands were on her, slipping something beneath her cheek so her face was not on the dark, damp soil of the forest floor, his voice crooning to her, as if she were a sick child or injured animal.

These small considerations touched her, made her want to cry, but instead she curled up tighter still. Breathed deep.

The dizzy feeling was abating. She looked up, saw him hovering over her, and struggled to sit up.

"What happened?"

His face was difficult to make out in the dark, but she sensed his hesitation.

"Tell me. I felt so sick."

He brushed a pine needle from her hair. "That was what some call the Evil of the Forest."

"It was here? That's what made me ill?" She sat up straighter, leaned against the tree. "How are we still alive?"

"It's not like that. It can kill, but usually it . . . plays. Twists things from what they were. It's capricious, but not always cruel."

"You've seen it before? What does it look like?" She wondered why she hadn't seen it. She felt the cold brush of fear at what might have been done to her by the bogey man of the woods. The reason no one with a sound mind ever entered the Great Forest.

"Have you ever seen a fireball?" He did not sit, but remained crouched, ready, and she realized the danger had not past.

She nodded. "During bad thunderstorms. When lightning strikes and the earth does not absorb it. Balls of fire, racing across the ground."

"What people call the Evil of the Forest is like that, but not created from lightning. We can thank bastards like Eric the Bold for it." He stilled, listening, then turned to her again. "When sorcerers unleash too much power, they cannot channel it all. They create pockets of wild magic, like fireballs, racing away, absorbing, feeling, affecting the world."

"So it's not conscious? Not a living being?"

"It's a being." He lowered his voice. "It dissipates very slowly, leaving traces of itself behind. Strange things that shouldn't be. And I can sense it thinking, moving with purpose."

"And why do these balls of wild magic only exist in the Great Forest?"

"It took me a long time to find out." The look on his face was of stone. "The sorcerers send them here, instantly banish them as they are formed. They are dangerous. As dangerous to those who made them as to everyone else. The Great Forest has become the refuse ditch of the sorcerers of the Middleland."

She was silent as she absorbed what he'd said, readjusted years of thinking on the nature of the Evil of the Great Forest. She'd always imagined it a sorcerer. A monster of some kind.

Rane rubbed a hand over his face. "The wild magic that just paid us a visit is newly formed. Vital and strong. I think we can thank Eric for it. No doubt it was formed when he created that cursed glass mountain."

"Thank the heavens it passed us by, then." Kayla shivered.

As she spoke, someone started screaming. High pitched, desperate screams that flayed her nerves.

Rane ignored them, did not even turn toward the sound. He watched her, a strange look on his face. "What makes you think it passed us by?"

CHAPTER 8

"*D*jan or Holt just ran into it." Rane stood, braced and ready for action, although there was nothing he could do. Nothing he could ever do when faced with wild magic.

He still did not know why it left him unchanged. How he could feel it, find its treasures.

It seemed drawn to him, like a cat finding the one person who doesn't like them to rub against. He and Soren had always been able to sense wild magic, and somehow endure its interest unscathed.

He'd felt it touching Kayla, arm-thick bands of power, curious and ruthless, that had slipped past his protection like a long-limbed sea monster, even as he willed it away. Willed his body broader.

She seemed unharmed. Unaffected. But it had lifted her up, turned her this way and that as if viewing a strange toy from every angle.

He'd seen an old woman turned young and beautiful, and mad with it. Seen a tree grow legs and skulk off into the dark forest, confused with its new life.

Strange creatures that should not, could not, be.

He did not want to think what was happening to Djan or Holt.

They knew the dangers of the forest as well as he did. Had heard his and Soren's tales. Knew what had happened to their father—

The screaming cut short, as sudden as running into a door.

"If it didn't pass us, if it knows we're here, why aren't we screaming, too?" Kayla pushed herself up to stand next to him.

"I don't know."

She shuddered, her whole body involved, and bent to pick up her pack. "Let's move away. In case it decides to come back for us."

And in case whatever Djan or Holt had become was even worse than two thugs out to steal from them. He should really see what had become of them. There were hours yet until daylight, and he didn't want any nasty surprises.

"Let's go." He picked up the saddlebags.

"Where?" She whispered, slinging both their packs over her shoulder.

"I want to see what happened to Djan and Holt. We can go back to the camp, depending . . ."

"Depending on what?"

"Depending on whether they're still a threat."

She said no more, and he started forward, bending to scoop up a short, thick stick.

A sound, a horrendous, gut-clenching sound, suddenly rose up from just ahead. A gibbering, like a strange animal or person gone insane.

Rane turned, saw Kayla frozen in place. Even in the darkness he made out her wide eyes.

"Stay." He mouthed the word, not wanting to risk even a whisper. With infinite care, he lifted the saddlebags off his shoulders and gently set them down. He breathed in deep. Slipped the moonstone out of his pouch and clenched it in his hand. Only knowing he was now invisible helped him take a step forward. Then another.

When the sound was just a bush away, he crouched, moving slowly and carefully around to the right.

Djan's torch lay on the ground, still burning.

Illuminating a nightmare.

KAYLA SANK DOWN, remembering in time to set their packs gently on the ground. Rane had moved faster than she'd expected. She could no longer see him.

Then she heard him, his footsteps heavy and without caution as he ran straight toward her.

And still she could not see him.

The footsteps were almost on top of her when suddenly he winked into sight, and she could not help her scream of surprise.

"I forgot. Sorry, I forgot." He hauled her to her feet, his face tense. He turned back the way he'd come. Listened.

The gibbering noise had stopped, and the bush rustled.

Rane did not wait to pick up the bags, he dragged her away, straight into the forest. The sound of branches snapping, of leaves crushed underfoot followed them.

Something large was after them, and the gibbering noise started up again. This time gleeful, rather than confused.

"What is it? *What is it?*" Kayla didn't dare look back, her focus on the ground before her. On not tripping in the dark.

Then Rane stopped and she smacked into him, fell to the ground.

She started scrambling back to her feet when she saw why he'd come to a halt. A ball of purple-green light was just in front of them. It shifted and moved, blocking their path.

Whatever was following them stopped, too, and at last Kayla turned back to see. For the second time that night she felt bile rise in her throat.

It was a thing. A creature of stone and soil, dead leaves and wood. But it was human, too. Two sets of eyes, one where a head should have been, the other lower down the abdomen. They gleamed with madness. Eight limbs stuck out of it, a bizarre mixture of arms and legs. One of the hands held a double-sided axe.

It seemed as interested in the wild magic as it was in them, the eyes shifting from one to the other.

Beside her, Rane swore, an expletive she'd only ever heard on the knights' training field.

"I'm going to disappear again. Try to draw it off." He vanished even as he spoke, and though she could still feel him standing beside her, she felt deserted and alone.

Then he moved, not away from the beast but toward it. She heard his fingers scrabbling on the ground.

Sand. He was going to throw sand in its eyes.

As the sand struck it, it bellowed, a deep, whistling sound. The sound she imagined the forest would make, if it had a voice.

Neither of them expected it to move so fast, but it thrashed out at Rane even though it could not see him, and Kayla heard him shout with pain, heard the heavy thud of his landing.

Without waiting, without any hesitation at all, the thing came for her, screaming as it did, axe raised.

Kayla turned desperately to the wild magic, willed it to distract what it had made, willed it to move. Then she spun back, saw the monster falter, then stop.

There was a crackle, a snapping of static in the air, and the wild magic rolled past her and slammed into the Djan-Holt-thing. It exploded in a horrific rain of man and decomposing forest.

She hunched over, curled up to protect herself against the pieces thrown back toward her.

Her head spun.

She had willed the wild magic to stop its monster. And it had.

CHAPTER 9

*T*he nagging sense of urgency had returned, stronger than before, and Kayla guessed it was because they'd gone back to the camp. The enchantment did not like retreat.

She looked down at her hands, shaking with nervous energy, and rubbed them against her thighs to still them. Enchantment or no, neither she nor Rane had slept, and they couldn't go on without rest.

She sat on her pallet, and tugged off her boots.

"It's fortunate the wild magic moved when it did." Rane was watching her, she could feel his eyes, but she concentrated on her boots, letting her hair swing over her shoulder to shield her face. She didn't want him to see her confusion.

Had she directed the wild magic's behavior?

"Yes," she said at last. "Very fortunate."

"I didn't expect that thing to move so fast." His voice was flat. "I'm sorry I left you in such a vulnerable position."

She blinked. Looked at him at last. This was an apology? He was crouched beside the fireplace, and his face was haunted. His fingers traced the handle of the knife he'd disappeared for ten minutes to find, the movement distracted, as if he thought he'd have to draw it at a moment's notice.

"You could hardly help it. You ran right at it to draw it off." Despite how she felt about him, about how he'd lied to her, the moment he'd turned invisible and ran at the thing to throw sand in its eyes, she'd known he was a man of honor. He could have slipped, invisible, into the dark of the forest and left her to her fate too many times for her to believe anything else.

It made what he'd done both harder and easier to accept.

At last, he turned to the small pile of sticks they'd collected and coaxed the flames to life. The crackle of the fire had never been so welcome.

She lay down and closed her eyes, felt the heat of the fire dance across her eyelids. "How does Eric not know about you?"

"Know about me?"

She was too tired to open her eyes and read his expression. "He didn't sense any magic in you. But you can disappear."

There was silence, and Kayla almost drifted off to sleep waiting for his answer.

"I'm no sorcerer. But I have access to magical objects."

"Mmm?"

"I find magical objects. I sell them."

"That's how you make your living?" She finally opened her eyes, but he wasn't looking at her. He was busy with the fire again.

"I trained as a knight for Jasper, but we . . . couldn't see eye to eye, and I went back to my family's business. I'm a woodsman."

"And you find magical objects while you're cutting down trees?" She could not help the disbelief in her voice.

"You saw what wild magic can do." He looked across at her. "It can make beautiful things as well as terrible. Imbue them with the most amazing powers."

"So you hunt for these things in the woods?" She sat up, looking at him over the flames.

He nodded and her heart picked up its pace. She didn't feel as tired any more.

"You find them, and some you sell?"

He lifted his head. "Most I sell."

He was warning her. Reminding her he was a working man. No prince. And one with a strange employment, at that.

"So what is it that turns you invisible?"

He put his hand in his pouch and drew out a shimmering moonstone, flat on one side, rounded on the other. It glowed like moonlight on his palm.

"If I close my hand over it, and rub it with my thumb, I disappear." He made a fist and she saw his thumb move and suddenly he wasn't there. Then he was back, stone sitting once more on his open palm. "It comes in useful."

"So you're not a knight of Jasper's stronghold." She paused a moment. "Or his secretary. You're a magic hunter." It made sense now. "And the magic you were hunting this time was the golden apple."

He said nothing, but he looked straight into her eyes.

She held her breath and everything else fell away. For a moment, it was just him and her, and an ocean of unspoken words between them. Of kisses not yet given, touches not yet felt.

She blinked, and tried to remember what they were talking about. He had no right to look at her like that. So full of regret and desire.

"I am sorry." He lifted an arm, as if to touch her, but dropped it back at his side.

She wanted to cry, to rage, to accuse, but she refused to do it again. Her father had wearied her of that game when he'd put her up as a prize to be won.

She found a place of calm within. Found the strength to be steady and unaffected. She had used him, too. Had had her own agenda that night. And although she had been honest in her motives, where he had not, she would not point fingers.

"How does your brother fit into this?" Her voice came out as she wanted. Cool.

She would not lay herself open and vulnerable to him again so easily.

She saw a look on his face—pain. It should have made her feel better, but it didn't.

"Jasper has my brother prisoner. His ransom is the golden apple."

"And you are sure Jasper will harm him?"

He laughed, the laugh of the wind through bare winter trees. "Jasper will kill him with relish if I give him even the slightest excuse."

"Why?"

Rane's eyes narrowed. "It's a long story. Believe me, Jasper hates Soren. He hates me, too, just not quite as much. And he knows I won't work for him any more. The only way he could get me to acquire the apple was to force me."

"But why you? Why not use someone else, and still kill your brother, if he wants to so badly?"

"Because magic is drawn to me. If anyone could have gotten that apple it was me." He closed his eyes. "Or Soren. Magic comes to him, too."

"So you can do this? Get the jewel for Eric?"

He shrugged. "If the jewel were hidden in the forest, or was part of a challenge, I would definitely get it. But the jewel belongs to someone. I have never stolen before."

Ah, but that was not true. She thought of what he'd stolen from her. Her trust. She breathed deep against the sudden pain and flopped onto the pallet, looked up at the clear, star-rich sky. "So Eric's plan worked perfectly. He's found a magic hunter to get his jewel."

At last, Rane sat on his own pallet. She saw him lie back and fold his arms under his head. "And every day it takes me to get it, my brother dies a little more."

"And we go a little more mad," she whispered back.

"WHERE ARE WE?"

Rane pulled up short as Kayla stopped and turned to him. She'd barely spoken since they'd begun their journey into the heart of the forest, and her voice was rough, unused to speech.

"Heading north. More than that, I don't know." He'd felt her agitation for the last hour, maybe more. She was walking slower, looking at where they were. Looking back at him.

Her looks were cool.

His attempt to apologize last night had not cleared the air. He hadn't expected it to, but he preferred the fiery anger he'd seen in her yesterday to this quiet disappointment. That he deserved it made it no less palatable.

Having her in front of him all day, her hair tied back so he could see the delicate nape of her neck and a hint of the smoothness of her back, had aroused him far more than any woman he'd ever seen naked.

He had been fantasizing about taking the long stride that would bring him up against her, anchoring her to him around her waist and lowering his head, breathing in the scent of her before kissing that pale golden skin.

"What?"

Her voice was like the chop of an axe on stone. He jerked. She had stopped, and was standing facing him with a hand on her hip.

"What do you mean, what?"

"What are you thinking?

He made his face blank. "It's near sunset. We need a little more haste. I want to find a good clearing to settle in for the night."

She narrowed her eyes. "We haven't passed a single clearing since we started out this morning."

"We've passed three. One on our right, two on our left."

"Oh." She hunched her shoulders, suddenly wilting, and the packs dropped with a thump. He hoped the golden apple was robust. "Will it come again? The wild magic?"

"I don't know."

With a sigh, she picked up the packs and looped them back on her shoulders. Turned to the path and continued on, her pace faster.

The path kinked right, twisting sharply, and she disappeared from sight for a moment. Even this small loss of contact jolted him, made him uneasy, and he took quick, long strides and slammed into the back of her.

Just as in his fantasy, he was forced to grab her around her waist, but it was to keep her from falling, not to make love to the back of her neck.

Her eyes were fixed ahead, and he followed her gaze, his heart sinking.

The weariness, the helplessness that he felt more and more when coming across the cruel jokes of wild magic, settled over him like the dust motes floating in the sunlight in the clearing ahead, swirling and falling, clinging to his skin, his clothes, his whole body.

A woman sat before them, beautiful beyond anything, placed exactly in a beam of light let in by a gap in the tall trees. She had long blonde hair that spilled over her shoulders, down onto her lap and came to rest just over her knees. Her dress was a pale blue, the back skirt longer than the front, so when she walked it would form a train, although now it draped prettily, perfectly, along the base of the tree stump she was sitting on.

But there was something wrong.

Of course there was something wrong.

A fly, black, grotesque, danced across her cheek, then dipped into her left eye, rubbing its little hands with glee.

And the woman did not brush it away. Did not blink. She did nothing, her hands serene and calm in her lap.

But her eyes.

They snapped and sparked, as alive as the rest of her was dead.

Kayla made a sound in the back of her throat, a cry and a sob in one. She twisted in his arms, lifting her face to his, and the horror of what she was feeling was in every line.

Perhaps that is how he looked, once. It must have been.

"Who is that?" Her whisper was loud in the still air.

Rane shook his head. "I don't know. It could once have been a rabbit, or a mouse, a real woman, a stone. There is no way to tell."

"We must do something."

MICHELLE DIENER

He had felt that too, long ago. Now he knew better.

He shook his head, and started walking on. "We can do nothing."

CHAPTER 10

$\mathcal{S}$ he came closer to hating Rane De'Villier, truly hating him, with every step they took away from the clearing. Even though she knew it wasn't his fault, even though she could suggest nothing to help the woman, his stoic acceptance of their helplessness made her wild with anger.

The clearing was perfect for their needs, just what they had been looking for, and she wanted to stay. To talk to the woman, perhaps ease her torment a little. Even though the thought of sleeping with those eyes watching, snapping—on the verge of madness or already well over the other side, made her uncomfortable, she would have borne it. To sit suspended, and completely aware, would drive most people insane, and what was a little discomfort compared to that?

"I used to feel the same."

Rane's words were so unexpected, she stumbled.

"Did you?" She spoke as if spitting something sour from her mouth.

He was silent, and she turned to look at him over her shoulder. And stopped dead.

Pain was etched so deep in his eyes, her heart hurt. His fists were clenched, and shame engulfed her, hot and burning as a shaft of midday sun through the trees. What did she know of him, of what he'd seen and felt?

He worked this forest. Knew more about wild magic than all her father's court put together.

What would that do to someone? Coming across things distorted or changed, and time and again being unable to put it right.

"I'm sorry. I have no right to be angry with you." Her apology was soft, and at the sound of her voice he seemed to shake himself free of his torment.

"I'm sorry, too. I know how hard it is."

They faced each other and the moments ticked by, until the swish of the wind through the leaves and the damp, musty scent of wet earth and mushrooms pressed against her senses. She felt as frozen in place as the woman in the clearing; she wanted to move, to turn back to the path, but her feet would not obey.

He took a step forward, and inwardly she flinched. She could not get lost in him again. She would never find her way back.

The first time, she'd thought she was in control. The user rather than the used. And even then he'd made her forget the reason she'd invited him to her chamber. The means had become an end in itself. She had put aside everything, lived truly in the moment.

And the next day the moment was exposed as a lie.

He was going to press his lips against hers, hold her to him—his every step forward told her he would, and she could not allow it. There would be no illusions, no hiding from the feelings he could draw effortlessly from her if she did.

Her fear at what would happen, what his kiss might confirm, finally gave her the strength to turn away. She would rather not know the truth.

Rather not know if Rane De'Villier had stolen her heart.

SHE WAS NOT SNEAKING.

Sneaking would mean Rane De'Villier held some power over her, and he did not.

Kayla looked over her shoulder, back toward the camp, and decided her growing unease was the enchantment at work again.

It had shown before it did not like retreat, and as she walked back down the path the way they'd come, it clung to her like a goblin, with claws dug into her chest and a stranglehold on her throat.

She fought against it as she made her way back to the woman in the clearing.

A breeze picked up, fluttering the flame on the burning stick she held for light, and for a moment she was in almost total darkness.

Her torch flared to life again, and she stopped, breathing hard.

She could not get the woman out of her mind. The thought of being frozen in a living statue, the hell of that existence, shook her to her core. It ate at her peace of mind, until she could no longer stand it.

Even the enchantment, making her jittery and panicked, could not stop her. Rane's orders certainly couldn't.

If it were her, she would have died a little to see people draw back from her and walk on without a word. If it were her, she would want some conversation at least, some small diversion.

If that was all Kayla could do for the woman, then so be it. It was something. More than De'Villier was prepared to do.

She had left him sleeping, and she was sure if he had heard her moving, taking a stick from the fire, he'd think it was for nothing more than a call of nature.

A twig snapped nearby, through the undergrowth, and Kayla started. She was still standing on the pathway, and she had a strange feeling more time had passed than she thought. It must be fatigue and the weight of the enchantment.

She strained her ears for another sound, but there was none and she moved again, down the path toward the clearing.

The wind rose up again, scattering leaves in her path, sending the branches above her rattling into each other and hissing as they shook their pine needles.

Kayla cocked her head.

She could have sworn she heard a more deliberate rustle, but the wind rose stronger, strong enough to lift leaves in an intricate dance before her.

And there was the clearing just ahead.

Kayla's feet slowed.

Her heart bled for the woman, for the horror of her life, but still, shamefully, she was afraid of her, too. The strange mix of pity and fear she'd felt for a dancing bear that had come to the castle with the fair once.

It had lain slumped on the ground, still as a statue, tethered to a stake. Even though it could not break free, even though she stood too far for it to reach her if it tried, fear pumped through her as she'd watched it, along with a soul-deep sorrow.

The woman's predicament, and her eyes, alive with rage, had reminded Kayla of the bear. Reminded her of its aura of violence suppressed, and denied. Seething just below the surface, ready to leap at the slightest chance.

Kayla shivered. Made her feet move forward again.

She stepped through the trees into the clearing, and in the second before the wind blew her flame out, she saw something that made her heart leap and twist in her chest.

The woman was gone.

CHAPTER 11

*S*he thought he would let her go off in the forest alone? She thought he was *asleep*?

Rane didn't know what to make of that.

Didn't know what to make of her. This princess who was somehow his betrothed.

He'd responded with bravado to her father at Gaynor Castle, asserting his rights to her to get them moving, because he'd foreseen days of delay if he hadn't insisted on leaving immediately, but he hadn't truly believed what he'd said.

Though saying it had felt like an oath to protect her.

She was his by law, and yet, he knew she was not his at all. She was no-one's but her own.

He couldn't sleep. Not with her tossing and turning beside him. With the thought of the kiss he had not taken hovering between them, as tantalizing as it was crazy.

She had been about to let him. He'd seen the quick dart of her tongue to her lips, the swallow of her throat, the way her lips parted, softly, sensuously.

And then, like the slam of a door, she'd turned. Pretended the moment hadn't existed.

He stood from his pallet, checking the fire to make sure it was safe to leave it.

She was returning to the woman in the clearing, and that puzzled him. He understood the horror of it—if she only knew how well he understood. How personal his experience was in this.

But what did she think she could do?

It was almost as if she were drawn to the woman by something outside of herself. Some additional enchantment. She had walked into the clearing first, after all.

At that thought, he started down the path at a faster pace than he'd planned, the moonstone firmly in his palm. She was nowhere to be seen, and he cursed.

He'd waited too long.

It was a mistake he wouldn't make with her again.

He ran, taking the path in long, loose strides. The wind was stronger now, and the rustle and scratch of the leaves and the tapping of branches hid most of his noise.

It was taking too long, as if the distance between their camp and the clearing had been altered, lengthened; and in this forest, he didn't discount it.

Where was she?

When the first streaks of panic began to fizz through his blood, he saw her. Just ahead, holding a branch with a wavering flame. She walked reluctantly, and he wondered again if it was against her will, if she was compelled.

She stepped into the clearing, out of view but for the weak glow of her makeshift torch, and Rane heard her exclaim in shock and horror.

Then the flame was extinguished.

Rane sped faster, flying into the clearing and stopped just before he slammed into Kayla.

She felt him, heard him, and turned, looking straight through him, her eyes wide. "Who's there?"

Her voice trembled.

He felt the weight of the moonstone in his hand, was about to open his fist, when a tinkling laugh came from behind her.

Kayla spun back. "Are you there? Are you free at night?"

A light began to throb and glow, just within the trees, and then the woman stepped into the clearing, her dress somehow glittering, as if threaded with starlight.

"You came to see me?" Her voice was at odds with her beautiful face, hard and cold.

Rane saw Kayla flinch at the sound, take a small step back. He moved out of her way.

"I wanted to see if I could help." She spoke softly, her hands clasped before her. "I could not get your fate out of my head."

"And who are you?"

"Kayla of Gaynor."

His princess stood taller. Drew herself up.

"And the man with you earlier? Who is he?"

She was still a long time, and Rane felt the bite of curiosity.

"My betrothed."

Rane almost dropped the moonstone.

"A prince and a princess wandering through the Great Forest." The woman laughed, trill and high, as pure and icy as the starlight glittering from her clothes. "What am I to do with you?"

Kayla frowned, and she stepped forward, this time, not back. "Do?" She unclasped her hands. "Can you run from here, or do you always end back in this clearing during the day?"

"I become a statue wherever I am when the sun rises. And I chose this clearing, so deep in the Great Forest, because I find if I am closer to the edges, where there is more chance of meeting people, the men . . . are not as respectful of my person as you and your betrothed were today." The woman looked straight at Kayla. "Not respectful at all."

Kayla made a sound, a cry of outrage. "If it were in Gaynor, please tell me where and who, and I will make sure they are punished."

The woman laughed again, softer this time. "Not Gaynor, but thank you, little princess. No one has offered me recompense before."

"Who are you? Where are you from?" Kayla crossed her arms below her breasts and shivered in the wind.

"I don't know." The hardness was back. "I cannot remember another life than this."

"Was it the wild magic?"

The woman cocked her head, genuinely puzzled. "Wild magic?"

Kayla looked over the woman's shoulder, unable to speak, and Rane saw what had frozen her tongue. Wild magic, smaller than the ball of energy from last night, rolled out from the trees behind the woman. It seemed to spin in place, and yet, to be completely still.

Looking at it too long made his eyes water.

Kayla pointed, mute, and the woman turned slowly.

"My pet." She crowed in delight, reaching down a hand to stroke the flaring ball of energy.

It contoured to her hand, pressing up against her like a cat.

"The men who hurt me?" The woman spoke with a purr, as if she took on the behavior of the wild magic. "I don't need recompense for what they did. I dealt out justice every night, all by myself." She patted the wild magic. "With a little help."

Kayla moved at last, backing toward the path to their camp.

"Stay a while." The woman smiled. "Or don't you like my pet?" She lifted her hand from it. "I was thinking what I could do with you and your prince."

Kayla seemed unable to take the final step that would get her out of the clearing. Rane stepped behind her, ready to physically push her.

"Perhaps you would make good love birds." The woman dipped her hand into the wild magic, and faster than Rane anticipated, faster than seemed possible, she threw a handful of energy at Kayla.

Rane leapt, pushing Kayla down, out of the way, but he was too late, too slow. The purple-green light sped quicker than a blink, hit her full square, and as he fell beside her he braced for something terrible, his heart hammering in his throat.

But instead of changing her, hurting her, it rebounded off her, spinning back toward the woman.

"It's me," he breathed in Kayla's ear, scrambling up and dragging her to her feet. "Run."

She looked straight at him, as if the moonstone was no longer in his hand, and she could see his eyes.

"Run!"

The woman screamed, and Kayla, at last, ran from the clearing. He saw her stumble on the path, right herself, and disappear into the night.

Then he turned to the woman. The wild magic she'd thrown at Kayla broke over her like a spray of water from a wagon wheel. She cringed back, and it danced in the air over her head.

The air wobbled like jelly, rippling over her, and the woman was not beautiful any more. She was middle-aged, with a spiteful mouth, thin and down-turned. Her clothes hung from her, dirty rags, and her hair was limp and string-like.

She stared down at herself and shrieked, her hands going to her mouth, the knuckles standing out sharply against the thin, white skin.

She looked at the wild magic, and Rane felt a shiver of fear at the hatred in her.

He could not leave this woman loose in the forest. She would try to harm them.

"You betrayed me, pet. You turned against me." She dug her arms deep into the wild magic, lifting up an armful of flickering energy. "Let us have another try, eh? Find the princess and her prince."

She laughed, the sound as chilling as the mad giggling from the Djan-turned-monster the night before. She took a step across the clearing, and the wild magic fell from her grasp, liquid as water through her fingers. It pooled on the ground beside her and flowed back to the spinning ball.

"What? You will not? I'll do it myself, then." She bent, picked up a rock. Hefted it in her hand, her eyes on the path to their camp.

Rane tensed. Could he kill a woman?

The wild magic moved, a gentle roll across the ground,

connecting with the woman's back and legs, leaping up to engulf her completely.

She fell hard to the ground, crying out. And was gone.

Rane stared at where she had been, his body tight with adrenalin.

The wild magic spun, moved a little in Rane's direction and seemed to look at him, focus on him, despite the moonstone clutched in his hand. Then it rolled out of the clearing the way it had come in and disappeared among the trees.

Rane realized his hands were shaking.

What had it done with the woman? He stepped closer. Saw something small move at his feet.

It was a frog, blinking up at him with yellow eyes.

He crouched down beside it. "As it happens, I'm no prince."

CHAPTER 12

$\mathcal{K}$ ayla ran halfway to the camp and stopped. Turned back.

No matter what may happen, she would not cower by the fire while Rane dealt with the woman and wild magic. Dealt with a situation of her own making.

He had protected her since they'd begun this journey, and she would not repay him by leaving him to face danger alone.

She walked back quickly, her shoulders and neck stiffer with every step as the enchantment made its displeasure known, her hands clenched in fists to stop them shaking.

A flicker of light to her right slowed her feet, and wild magic was suddenly in front of her on the path. Blocking her way.

She could not make a sound, her heart stuttering in her chest, her ears ringing. She could do nothing but stare.

It rose up, stretching itself, forming a huge oval, like the cheval mirror in the corner of her room in Gaynor Castle.

The green-purple light flickered and thinned, but she could not see through it to the forest beyond. Instead, she was looking into some other place, like a pool reflecting back a different reality.

She leaned forward and made out a stone staircase, rising upward, a single sconce lighting the way.

Then she heard a sound. Not from the forest, but from within the image before her – footsteps, coming down the stairs. The tread was quick, energetic. Masculine.

Fear gripped her. She had a terrible sense whoever was coming would see her. Would be able to step out of the magic into the forest with her.

She moved back, but the wild magic moved with her.

"No," she whispered. But instead of obeying her, like it had before, it moved again, straight at her.

For a moment there was a strange sense of nausea, a sparkle of light around her.

Then Kayla shivered.

She was standing at the bottom of the steps in an icy, dark chamber, the smell of cold, damp stone filling her nose. And the footsteps were coming closer.

She spun around. The oval shimmered, an open window back to the forest in the otherwise impenetrable darkness of the room. Through the wavering light she saw the trees, the path. And though every step she'd taken in the forest had been one of fear, she wanted nothing more than to fling herself through the strange doorway, back to the familiar.

The footsteps behind her stopped, and she turned slowly, her pulse thundering in her ears.

Eric the Bold stared at her, the shock on his face so clear, so sharp, she knew for certain he had nothing to do with this strange doorway between the forest and himself.

He made a noise, a gurgle, as if trying to speak, and then shook his head, cleared his throat. "What are you doing here?"

"Where am I?"

"My stronghold. In my dungeons."

She thought he would step closer, but he did not, staying on the second last step. His eyes flicked from the wild magic, back to her.

"I wonder why it brought me here?" Kayla reached out a hand, casually, as if making nothing more than a gesture, and her hand slipped through the curtain of light. She could feel the warmer air of the forest on the back of her hand, the gentle stroke of the wind. Would it let her back through?

"It . . . brought you?" Eric scowled.

"I certainly didn't have anything to do with it." Kayla turned back to him, drawing herself up.

"That is very interesting. I wonder . . ." Eric extended a hand, as if she should take it. Come closer to him.

She did not move.

Fast as the viper he was, he stepped forward and grabbed her wrist, jerking her back with him to the stairs. He held her close, close enough for her to smell the curious mix of herbs and wood smoke on him. But underlying it all, there was something else. The cold, sour smell of deep, dark places.

Kayla looked down at where his hand manacled her wrist, and then up at his face.

There was a flush of color on his cheeks, and he was breathing hard. "Perhaps you were thinking of me, hmm? Perhaps that's why you are here?"

Kayla jerked her arm, hard. "No."

"I have certainly been thinking of you." Eric tightened his grip, lifted his other hand and stroked her cheek.

Kayla flinched back.

"Not saving yourself for De'Villier, are you?" Eric smiled. "The heroic savior who was only after the apple, not the princess."

Kayla went still.

"I know about you, Kayla of Gaynor." Eric's words were sly. "I know the secret your father tried so hard to hide. My only mistake was underestimating the lengths he would go to keep you from me without showing his hand."

Her throat closed, and Kayla had to force out her response. "What do you know?"

Eric laughed. "How innocent you look. I must commend you, but witches are duplicitous, aren't they? You take after your kind so well."

"Witches." She repeated the word, flat and expressionless.

"Your dear, departed mother, of course, although like you she was untrained, and your paternal grandmother. With power from both sides, I've had my eye on you for quite some time. Your heritage shines out of you. But I cannot believe the restraint you've shown." He twisted her arm painfully, looking at her inner wrist, and shook his head. "I don't know if it's a sign of outstanding control, or total ineptitude. But we shall see, won't we?"

She stamped down on every emotion swirling within, every question, and forced her eyebrows up. Forced her words to be cool and biting. "What did you have in mind?"

Eric fingered a strand of her hair, pushed it off her face, and it took everything in her not to jerk away. "I think you can guess." He lowered his mouth to her ear. "You've been so obliging, turning away suitor after suitor, giving me time to build up my power. Then came De'Villier. He managed to impress you because he let you do the work, am I right? Let you think you were in control. But with me, you can have all the control you have ever wished for. More power than your father, more power than any other in Middleland."

How little he understood. "Power through you?" She let a little of the scorn she was feeling slip into her question.

"You are hardly going to harness it on your own. I know you are . . . uninitiated." He gave the word a sexual innuendo. He dipped his head even lower, nuzzled her throat, leaving her gasping for breath at her vulnerability. She could feel the edge of his teeth, just beneath the softness of his mouth.

"The world will be at your feet." His whisper teased the shell of her ear, and she shivered.

His hand still held her wrist as viciously as before. The warm, gentle touch of his lips and the steel of his grip deepened her sense of violation.

She lifted her own hand, touched his face to bring his eyes back to hers.

"Kiss me," she whispered.

He laughed, a throaty sound of triumph, and released her wrist at last, lifting his hands to her shoulders to draw her closer.

In that sliver of a moment she was unrestrained, she dropped straight down in a crouch, spun, and dived headlong through the wild magic doorway.

RANE APPROACHED the wild magic cautiously. He'd seen it glimmering ahead, and with a sense of inevitability, of foreboding, he made his way toward it.

It had formed a thin oval, like a mirror, and as he came closer, it spun, so he was presented with the thin, almost invisible, side view.

The movement was furtive, as if it were hiding something from him. He moved right, and again it spun away.

Anger spiked in his chest, and he feinted right a second time, then leapt left. He found himself staring straight at a strangely lit Eric the Bold. Eric's head was thrown back, as if in triumph, but already, as Rane watched, he saw the beginnings of a frown.

He realized why a moment later, when Kayla of Gaynor leapt from the pale-green tinted image within the wild magic, into his arms.

The instant Kayla was through, the wild magic crumpled in on itself, forming its usual ball. It spun, lifted off the ground, and flew away.

Kayla struggled against him, and he realized he was holding her tight, as if Eric could lean through some magic window and grab her back. He set her down.

"What was that?"

She was breathing hard, her hands shaking. She lifted fingers to her forehead, and pushed back the hair that had fallen over her eyes.

He could see the dark red marks of a man's grip on her wrist.

"The wild magic. It formed that mirror thing and came straight at me. Sent me to Eric's dungeon."

She leaned over, hands on her knees and breathed deeply.

Rane was unable to say anything. Eric's dungeon?

Kayla lifted her head. "Eric was surprised. And scared." She straightened. "He wouldn't come near it."

"Why did he have that look on his face?" Rane saw her hands tug at her shirt, smooth back her hair.

"What look?" She glanced at him, but he knew she'd understood what he meant.

He didn't answer, kept his gaze steady on her.

She made a sound, exasperated. "He thought I'd decided to take what he offered."

"And what had he offered?" Rane realized he was knocking his fist hard against his thigh, and forced his arm still.

Kayla's eyes were serious, worried. "Everything." She spun away, began down the path back to the camp, but stopped after two steps. Turned. "And nothing."

She looked so stricken, so small, he understood there was more to it than that. Eric had done something to her. Told her something, or threatened her, and she was not going to tell him what.

With a curse, he strode forward, gripped her shoulders.

"What did he say to you?" He just resisted shaking her, forcing his fingers to hold her lightly.

He expected her to shout, or put on the cool, untouchable royal look she'd used since she realized he'd betrayed her. But she did neither.

Instead, a tear spilled from her eye, and ran down her cheek, and her lips trembled.

"What did he say to you?" He said it gently this time, let his hands fall from her shoulders.

She shook her head. Drew herself up. "He assumed I knew things . . . that I did not know. He could be lying, but I don't think so. If he's right, my parents lied to me, and kept things from me. But he doesn't know that, and so he thinks he understands me. That he knows what I want."

"And does he?" Rane stepped back, putting a little distance between them.

Her gaze flew to his, and held. She looked five years old. Lost.

"No." She took a step toward him, and suddenly she didn't look five years old any more. She lifted her face and her lips brushed his, light, tentative. "He doesn't understand me at all."

[faint text bleeding through from reverse side of page]

CHAPTER 13

*I*t was the kiss Kayla should have given Rane earlier. The kiss she had wanted but her pride and her caution had refused to let her take.

Eric thought she wanted power, but really, all she wanted was the right to determine her own path. And the only one who'd ever helped her with that was Rane.

His response, immediate, completely serious, set her whole body trembling with anticipation. She'd felt the full force of his concentration once before. Her body sang at the thought of receiving it again.

He did not hold her, did not touch her, the only point of contact was their lips.

It made her skin unbearably sensitive. Every brush of forest breeze, every flutter of her clothes, teased her.

When he stepped back, she thought it was to take her in his arms, but when she opened her eyes, he was staring at her, his face a tight mask.

"What is it?" She heard herself speak as if from far off, as if she were waking from a dream.

"What do you want from me?" His voice was stark, the deep timbre of it fraying at the edges.

"Want?" She blinked, feeling stupid.

"Whatever we did together that night in your chamber, whatever your father has given me right to, the fact remains, princess, I am a woodsman. What do you want of me?"

She could not recall ever being at such a loss. She brought her hands together, stared at her intertwined fingers. What did she want of him, specifically? "I don't know."

He said nothing, but his jaw bunched and his hands and arms were clenched so tight, she could see the muscles, the tendons, standing out.

The silence went on for a beat. Then another. At last, she turned and started back to the camp. She could feel his eyes on her, like an itch between her shoulder blades.

And running through her head with every step she took away from him was the thought that he was the only one to ask her what she wanted since this nightmare began.

RANE HAD ALWAYS BEEN the thinker, the calm, deliberate one in his family. The one who used his muscle only when necessary, his brains all the time. Soren had the hotter head, the more impulsive nature.

But now, Rane wished his brains to the darkest corners of hell.

Kayla walked ahead of him, just as she had last night, after he'd brought their kiss to an abrupt halt. Every swing of her hair, pulled into a thick tail hanging down her back, every sway of her hips in their blue cotton trousers, was a brutal reminder of what he could have had, if only he'd kept his mouth shut and let his heart take over from his head.

When he'd asked his question last night, she'd looked stricken. As if she'd betrayed herself.

He'd forced her to think far too much.

Now, even the easing of the enchantment, from a death grip to the firm, gentle hold of a lioness on her cub's neck, could not lighten either of their moods. At least they were nearing their goal. Rane did not believe the enchantment would give them this respite unless they were.

The wind picked up again, bringing a welcome stir in the hot air, mixing up the forest scents so the overriding smell in his nostrils was green.

It cooled the sweat on his arms and neck, but the rattle and hiss of dead leaves blowing, and the sigh and creak of the trees, was dangerous. Anything could approach them, unheard, over the waterfall of sound.

Wild magic was almost impossible to see in the faint gloom of the forest by daylight, and he'd felt eyes on them for the last half hour. He didn't even try to persuade himself he was mistaken.

Something leapt, sinister and dark, from a tree to their right.

Rane closed the distance between himself and Kayla before she could even cry out, stepping in front of her, his knife in his hand.

He did not look down at the blade, but he knew it glimmered in the gloom. It was one of the only reasons he had to be grateful to wild magic. His knife had saved his life more than once.

"What was it?" Kayla stepped out from behind him, and he saw she'd picked up a stick from the forest floor.

"Do we want to know?"

She shrugged. "It's been following us for a while."

Irritation tugged at him. "Why didn't you say something?"

She spared him a sideways glance. "You knew already. I saw you looking for it."

There was a flash of a dark body, flitting from one tree to another at ground level, and Rane knew whatever it was, it was fast and sleek.

They had only been standing still a minute or less, and already the enchantment clamped them with a heavier hold. Rane felt a sense of desperation rising in his chest, and he tried to shut it out. He needed all his wits in this.

The wind dropped, and silence settled on them like a down coverlet.

A bush rustled, and Rane tensed, moving forward, ready for anything.

Something jumped, not at him, but over him. He caught a glimpse of black fur, and he had the sense of it twisting in the air, like a cat.

Kayla screamed, and Rane spun, knife up, heart thundering.

It *was* a cat. A cat large enough to reach his hip. Not a panther or a lion, it looked like a house cat, a hundred times the size. And it had Kayla on the ground, a paw resting on her chest.

THE WAY IT HAD SPRUNG, the size of its paws, Kayla expected to be in pain, but the cat had pushed her down almost gently, its claws retracted.

The golden eyes staring at her lifted up to Rane. It spat at him, hissing, and the fur on its back rose up. It ended with a yowl in the back of its throat that went on and on. She thought it would leap at Rane and attack at any moment.

"Shh." The word came instinctively from her. "Shh."

The terrible grumble stopped, and the cat looked back at her, curious.

Kayla pushed at its paw and it released her, sitting back as she stood. She reached out a hand, and scratched it under its chin.

The purr, when it came, was almost deafening.

"You're just lonely, aren't you, puss?"

Rane took a step closer, and when the cat did not react, sheathed his knife. "Don't encourage it."

Kayla frowned. "I thought I was saving us from being ripped to shreds."

He raised a brow. "You saved it from me. Now we have the problem of what to do with it."

She looked at him, the way he stood, easy and sure, and realized he was serious. He had no doubt he would have killed the cat. For some reason, that confidence, that bone-deep certainty, made her shiver.

"Well, I'm glad you didn't hurt it." She rubbed its flank. "It isn't to blame for what it's become."

She watched Rane move uncomfortably, and was suddenly aware of the same discomfort. She looked around for the bags she'd let fall, her mind turning to the path ahead, and cursed the enchantment.

"It feels stronger, doesn't it?" Rane was looking at her with a strange expression.

"Do you think we've gone wrong? Missed a path?"

He shook his head. "I think we're close. Close enough any little delay is punished."

Kayla gave the cat a last pat. "Sorry, puss, we have to go." She bent to pick up her saddlebag, and went flying with a cry as a head butted her back.

"Kitty wants to play." Rane's voice held laughter, and Kayla realized she'd never heard that lift in his voice before.

It was nice.

She picked herself up and brushed leaves and small twigs off her shirt and trousers.

The cat dipped her head and butted Kayla again. Even seeing it coming, she had to brace her legs to keep on her feet.

"We have to go." The laughter in Rane's voice had been replaced by desperation, and Kayla nodded. She was as on edge as he sounded, her nerves strung so tight, so quickly, she almost imagined Eric might be nearby, trying to control them.

She slung the bags over her shoulder, and Rane stepped aside for her to precede him.

Relief came with the first few steps down the path, and the imaginary goblin at her throat eased its hold.

There was a yowl of protest, and the cat moved, walking parallel to their path, winding through the trees. Kayla called to it, and it responded with a chirp. Its head whipped to the right and it pricked its ears, stopped dead. Then it sped away from them to the east.

Having a giant, playful cat with them would have made stealing the gem impossible, but Kayla was sorry to see it go.

She thought of what Eric had said, that she was a witch, and grinned. If he was somehow right, what a familiar that kitty would make.

CHAPTER 14

$\mathscr{R}$ ane smelled the wood-smoke nearly ten minutes before the path spat them out behind a dilapidated shed. Kayla stopped short, turning to look at him over her shoulder, her eyes wide. Questioning.

"I don't think this is it." He felt no ease of the relentless pressure of the enchantment.

He moved cautiously around the side of the shed, and a kick of surprise stopped him in his tracks. It was a small village.

The little cottages crowded along a strip of hard-packed earth, creating a rustic village square, protected on three sides. The houses were rough, wood and thatch, but the shutters were well-fitted and summer daisies and roses flourished in front of steep-pitched porches.

They were standing in a field, a large village green, which held a small herd of black-and-white cows. One of them had claw marks down its flank, and Rane thought immediately of Kayla's kitty.

A road, narrow but well-kept, snaked off to their left into the forest, in the direction of Therston.

He became aware of the silence, loud as a roar in his ears. The swish of the wind in the trees and the erratic bird song only accentuated the lack of human sound. In a village.

There was something very wrong here.

He jerked when Kayla touched his elbow. She pointed, and he noticed a figure standing just within a doorway, deep in shadow.

A door banged, and Rane swung in the direction of the sound. A man stepped out on a porch, breathing heavily, and Rane had the sense he had been working behind the house, perhaps cutting wood in the forest. He had been summoned to deal with trouble and he'd run every step of the way.

He had his axe in his hand, still edged with the green-brown skin of the tree he'd been chopping. He was a huge man, well-built and tall, but he held the axe as if prepared to do battle against monsters, not two travellers.

"Good day." Rane lifted a hand in greeting and started along the fence running beside the storage shed, toward the square.

"No further."

He stopped, and Kayla ran into his back, muttered something under her breath.

"We mean no harm. If you would prefer, we'll continue on now." The man lowered his axe. "Where are you from?"

"Gaynor." Kayla called out.

"Gaynor?" The axe sank a little lower. "What news from there?"

"The crops are good, the kingdom is peaceful." Kayla spoke what might as well have been the Gaynor motto.

"Aye? Can't say I've ever heard anything different about Gaynor. Although I'd have thought even it would have been affected by the current troubles."

"Troubles?" Rane took another step forward.

The axe came up. "How'd you get from the border of Gaynor to here without some consequences, eh? No one has stepped out onto our green from that path in the last half-year. No one human, that is."

"We've come across our share of horrors these last three days." Rane let his arms fall to his sides, palms out.

"Like?"

"Like a woman who was a statue by day, and a sorceress by night." Rane glanced at Kayla. "And a strange ball of light that made windows into other places. And a monster made of two men and the dead forest leaves."

"And a cat whose head came to my waist." Kayla stepped forward, to stand beside him.

"That would be Sooty."

"Sooty?" Kayla cocked her head.

"My daughter's cat. Or was. Can't say she's Sooty any more."

"I think she's probably still Sooty. Just bigger."

"I'm surprised you saw her and lived to tell the tale."

Rane could tell the woodsman was intrigued by their normal appearance. But the axe stayed raised. He thought of what he'd seen himself in the Great Forest and wondered that the man hadn't tried to kill them on sight, without stopping to question them.

"She just wanted to play." Kayla grinned. "And she likes being scratched under her chin."

At last, the axe lowered. "You're the luckiest pair I ever met, I'll give you that. Since the troubles began, we only see monsters this deep in. Most of us are planning to move."

Rane took his words to be an acceptance of them, and he started forward, easy and relaxed. "Do you know these parts well?"

The woodsman nodded, then snapped his head toward the path from Therston. Rane heard it, too, the sound of galloping, and put his hand on the hilt of his knife.

Behind them on the green, the cows began to low, deep, hair-raising bellows of fear.

A rider burst from the trees, cape flung back and flapping as his horse thundered toward them. He rode as if something was after him, and Rane saw, with a lightning strike of horror, something was.

A troll, stoop-shouldered and huge, lumbered after him; long nose and long hair sprouting from a massive head on a too-thin neck. In one hand it held a club.

The rider was coming at them so fast, Rane thought he was going to speed past them, back into the forest on the other side of the green, and leave them to face the troll alone. But just as he drew level, he reined his mount in, turning it with an elegant move that spoke of perfect accord between rider and horse.

Rane took a precious second to glance across as the rider freed his sword from its scabbard, and his eyes widened. He knew that sword.

There was no time to think about that, though. Instead, he drew his knife and focused back on the monster coming at them. The woodsman had joined them, and Rane realized the four of them had formed a loose defensive line.

Except Kayla had nothing to defend herself with. She didn't even have a stick.

The troll was making a sound, a sort of growl, as he saw his quarry run to ground, and three other tasty morsels besides. One reach of his long arms and Kayla would be gone.

There was nothing to do but attack. To reach the troll before it reached them.

"Get back." Rane didn't look to see if Kayla obeyed him. He ran forward and realized with surprise he was shouting—a long, continuous battle cry. The moonstone was in his left hand, and he closed his fist around it. Lifted his right hand, knife blade glimmering, lengthening, and leapt.

The blade slid into troll-flesh like it was soft butter. Rane slammed it in up to the hilt and pulled down, opening the troll's abdomen from lung to gut. Then he jumped back, out of the way, as the massive troll toppled.

It twitched, a feral stench rising from it, and he leapt back further, but it didn't move again.

Rane dropped the moonstone into his pack, and stood, breathing heavily, listening to the blood drip from his knife to the hard ground of the path.

The woodsman came up behind him and put a heavy hand on his shoulder. "Think I understand now how you got so lucky, coming through the forest."

"Oh, Mr. De'Villier is quite at home in the forest." A cool voice, a voice he knew, made him turn.

The horseman slid off his mount, sword still in hand, a smile on his face.

He would recognize that face anywhere.

"You know this man?" The woodsman looked between them.

"I do." At last, the man slid the sword back into its scabbard. "I'm his best customer."

THE TROLL LAY AS STILL and lifeless now as it had been vital and powerful before.

Kayla refused to sink to the ground, but that was what she wanted to do. Her whole body shook, tiny tremors she fought to control, and she clenched her fists to stop her hands betraying her to the others.

Rane stood braced, as if he expected the troll to rise up again at any moment, although his concentration was no longer on the troll, but on the strange horseman in flamboyant clothing, with a face that seemed neither young nor old.

What Rane had done—she couldn't stop seeing him run straight at the troll and then vanish as he leap up at it, knife raised high, over and over in her mind. She wondered if he wasn't somehow changed by the wild magic in a way he didn't realize. He had been so fearless. So sure. So focused.

Just as he'd been when he'd ridden up the glass mountain for the golden apple.

Kayla blinked, forced herself to concentrate on the conversation.

"Customer?" the woodsman was asking.

"De'Villier here sold me my sword. And a few other things."

"Jisuel." Rane inclined his head in the most minimal of nods.

The man Rane called Jisuel laughed, throwing back his head so his fine blond hair waved and curled down the back of his purple velvet cape. Kayla's eyes narrowed. There was something there, behind the laugh. Something she could almost grasp . . .

Suddenly she was caught in Jisuel's gaze, brown and green, the color itself a message of some kind. She struggled to break free, to tear away from that stare, knowing something was wrong, wrong . .
.

"Well, well."

She was released, and perversely, brought her eyes straight back up, held Jisuel's gaze again. She did not like feeling small and helpless. The troll had done it to her with its size and strength, Jisuel had done it with the force of his personality.

"I didn't know you worked with a partner, De'Villier. I thought your brother was your only companion." Jisuel's smile was considering and speculative.

Rane said nothing, standing exactly where he had since he'd brought the troll down.

"Bit deeper within the Forest than usual, aren't you? I thought you only worked the western border." Jisuel behaved as if Rane had responded to his earlier comment. Calm and relaxed, he could have been chatting to them over a mug of cider.

Again, Rane said nothing, and Kayla shifted uncomfortably. Saw the village woodsman do the same.

"Ah, well. You never were very talkative. I like that about you." Jisuel slipped a foot into a stirrup and swung himself up into the saddle. "I really must be off."

"Good to see you again, sir." The woodsman touched his forehead in an automatic gesture of fealty.

"Sorry about bringing that bit of excitement into your lives." Jisuel jerked his head at the troll. "Good thing Mr. De'Villier was around with his trusty knife and his death wish." There was an edge of contempt, a sneer, in his tone.

Rage cut Kayla off from the outside world. She was instantly dumb and blind.

She drew in a long, deep breath. "Don't you dare." Her voice shook as she spoke, and all three men turned surprised faces her way. "Apologize." She pointed a finger at Jisuel, amazed that it was rock-steady. "Apologize to Rane, now. To dismiss what he did as a death wish—" She had to swallow, to collect herself.

"You apologize or I will make you."

To her disbelief, Jisuel laughed, and her anger sparked, wild, at the edges of her control. The laughter died in his eyes, his gaze flicking to her fingers a moment. "I do apologize. I spoke flippantly, and it was disrespectful."

In a single, smooth move, he leapt from the horse and bowed deep and low to Rane. "You have quite a defender, De'Villier. Will you not both be my guests tonight? The inn in this village is no longer in use."

Kayla shuddered, her body releasing the tension of the last few moments. She felt . . . she *could* have made Jisuel apologize. She'd felt powerful. She met Rane's gaze over Jisuel's bowed head, and the shock in his blue eyes, the surprise, made her stomach lurch uncomfortably.

"I would like to buy supplies here first." Rane looked across at the woodsman, and he gave a quick nod. "We can join you later."

Jisuel straightened. "'Til later, then." He set his foot in the stirrup. "Gert will tell you the way."

He flung himself easily into his saddle, and cantered out of the village, the forest swallowing horse and rider with one great gulp.

"Where does Jisuel live?" Rane stared at the point where Jisuel had disappeared.

"Never been there myself but you follow the path north east a way." Gert turned back to the troll, and Kayla's eyes began to water as the stink of it filled her nostrils. "What are we going to do with this?"

"Jisuel will get rid of it." Rane crouched and cleaned his blade on a clump of grass.

Kayla looked at the massive body. "Can he?"

Rane met her disbelieving look. "Yes."

"Well, I'd appreciate it if he could." Gert swung his axe up onto his shoulder. "You want to buy some supplies, you said? Folks'll be pleased to get a bit of coin. We mostly trade in kind out here."

The woodsman started ahead of them, back to the cottages, and Kayla fell into step with Rane.

"Who is Jisuel?"

"Not someone to threaten. Not on my behalf." He sounded bemused, perplexed.

She recalled the look on his face when Jisuel had apologized. It had not been grateful. "I'm sorry if I've made trouble between you and your client."

He stopped, reached out a hand and grabbed her shoulder, swinging her to face him. "Don't be." He ran a hand through his hair. "No one has ever . . ." He stepped back, exasperated. "I don't know what to make of you."

She had no answer for him. She didn't know what to make of herself, either.

"You didn't realize, did you?"

She frowned. "Realize what?"

"When you told Jisuel to apologize or you would make him, there were wild magic sparks at your fingertips."

CHAPTER 15

$\mathcal{K}$ ayla must have some affinity to wild magic. Or it had done something to her, changed her in some way. The way it had been drawn to her, the sparkles of it on her fingertips, it made Rane sick with worry.

But even more worrying was that every step they took down the path toward Jisuel's home lifted the enchantment a little more. In spite of the heavy packs over his shoulders, Rane felt giddy with the lightness of it.

The creeping fear that Jisuel's house would be at the center of the forest, that the jewel they were to steal was his, slowed his steps.

Kayla, not knowing what Jisuel was, not understanding the implications, bounced eagerly down the path. She'd pulled far ahead of him already, singing under her breath.

"Kayla. Wait."

She must have heard the edge in his voice, because she stopped immediately, waiting for him to join her under a large tree.

"You feel it lifting, too?" She laughed. The first time he'd heard her laugh since the night he'd made love to her.

He cursed inwardly. That was not a memory to dredge up now. "I feel it. And it worries me."

She stilled. "Why?"

He found himself uncomfortably close to her, suddenly, on the narrow path. Found the stillness in her was a mirror of the forest.

They were utterly alone.

He fixed his eyes on the flushed skin at her collar-bone, just visible through her cotton shirt.

"We're nearing the end. And we are nearing Jisuel. That can mean only one thing."

"Jisuel is Ylana?" Kayla's voice was lower, suddenly hushed.

"Or Eric lied to us. Made Ylana up."

"Why would he do that?" She was whispering.

Rane hardly heard her, there was a buzz in his ears, and his body leaned forward, the packs on his shoulders dropping to his feet.

He bent his head, and as his lips touched her neck, the world stopped tipping. As long as he had her in his arms, had his hands and his mouth on her, the dizziness was gone.

"What is happening?" She spoke breathlessly, desire thick in her voice as he pressed her back into the tree.

"I have stopped trying to leave you alone."

She made a sound in her throat, a groan. "And I have stopped letting you."

He wondered why he'd let go of his control now, chosen this moment to forget the reasons he shouldn't do this. Why she had done the same. The question niggled at him, trying to douse some of his excitement, and he pushed it away, his fingers fumbling at the ties at Kayla's throat.

He opened her shirt, and gasped at the half-corset that held her breasts high and firm. His knees buckled and he needed the tree at her back to keep upright.

"What delightful thing is this?" He dipped his head lower, ran his tongue along the line where stiff cotton met soft skin.

Her breath hitched. "I could hardly wear nothing."

Well, she was a princess, after all. Something he tried to forget. Something that somehow made no difference at the moment.

He lifted her, his fingers curling around the top of her thighs encased in their blue cotton trousers, bringing her knees up to cage his hips.

Her breath came in gasps, her head back against the tree.

The world had slipped away, and there was nothing for him but the sound of her breathing, the heat of her, the feel of her skin beneath his fingertips.

She lifted half-closed eyes, languid and urgent at the same time, and then, like a splash of cold water, she blinked. Her gaze fixed on something beyond his shoulder, and with a rising sense of dread, Rane turned to look.

Wild magic spun, silent, ominous, just four feet behind them.

Holding Kayla steady, Rane set her back on her feet and stepped away from her. He turned, blocking her body with his own.

Waited.

He liked to *do*. To act, not react. But he could do nothing. Wild magic was not something he could control.

Behind him, Kayla shifted, then stepped out.

The magic reared up, rising like a wave hitting a rock, and rained over her, covering her in shimmering green and purple. She gave a cry, looked across at him, her eyes wide, and he reached out to grab her hand.

A shock, the pain bone-deep, snapped at him, throwing his hand up and back, and he saw part of the magic rise, as if to strike him again, like a snake.

He shoved the pain aside, ripped his knife from its sheath and stood, muscles bunched, teeth clenched. Ready for battle.

Helpless.

This could not be happening again. It could not take another from him.

A cry of frustration and fear tore from his throat.

Kayla was still, no longer looking at him but straight ahead, encased in rippling, transparent light. He tightened his grip on his knife, thinking to somehow shave the top layer of magic off, but as the thought formed in his mind, the glow thinned.

The magic fell from her and pooled at her feet, coalesced and rose up, a spinning sphere once more. It darted behind a tree and was gone.

Rane closed his eyes. He wanted to put off the moment of looking at her while he gathered his strength. Seeing her encased in wild magic had brought back the worst memory of his life, and he had to find the core of steel within to get him through whatever came next.

"What did you think it was doing to me?"

Her hand slid down his arm, tentative, and he flinched in surprise.

He snapped opened his eyes, and she was staring at him, biting her bottom lip. Perfect. Normal. Unchanged.

"I thought. . ." he had to clear his throat. "I thought it was trans-forming you into . . ."

He thought again of the way it coated her, like slime, and shuddered.

"Into what?"

"The same thing as my father."

SHE HAD FELT SOMETHING. A tug of . . . warmth, of interest. A feeling of belonging, and friendliness.

It worried her more than if she'd felt nothing, or pain. Why cover every inch of her body? What had the wild magic done to her?

Rane didn't help. He kept looking at her as if expecting her to grow another head or turn to stone, and irritation and fear made her hands jerky and her step clipped.

"What happened to your father?" She asked the question with a snap in her voice, turning to look at him over her shoulder.

"He's a piece of wood."

She fell, hard and badly, landing on her side and scraping her shoulder, her foot still caught and twisted in the root that tripped her.

Rane crouched beside her. "Are you all right?"

She nodded, wincing as she levered herself up. Bruised, scraped, but otherwise, unharmed.

"Wild magic turned your father to wood?"

He gave her an unreadable look. "We were working in the forest, my father, brother and I. My father cried out and we ran to him just as wild magic rolled right at him, through him. When it disappeared he was a wooden statue of himself. Well . . ." He hesitated. "Not a statue, really."

"What then?" She felt sick.

"A tree. It's been nearly two years, and he's begun to grow leaves in summer, on his head and along his arms and legs, like hair and clothing." He reached out for the packs she dropped, and she saw his hands were shaking. "It would be better if he were a carving. The way things are, I have the feeling he's still alive in there. Like that woman in the clearing. He might know what has happened to him. Perhaps he sees us when we visit him. Like her, he could be mad."

"Is that when you and Soren started hunting wild magic?"

He nodded. "At first, we thought to find it, beg it to change him back. But we realized soon enough it never would. It seemed completely uninterested in us. Never touched us. Never harmed us. And by following it, we found the things it created and left in its wake. We'd stopped chopping wood, and we'd both left Jasper's employ the year before. We needed to eat, so we started selling what we found."

She thought of her anger at him the night she'd gone back to the woman in the clearing, and felt the heat of shame on her cheeks. "What happened next?"

"I was away, selling what we'd found—to Jisuel—and Soren discovered how wild magic is formed. He'd always said it must be to do with Nuen, Jasper's sorcerer brother, and he started watching Nuen's rooms at night, sneaking into Jasper's stronghold. He discovered wild magic was created in the aftermath of wielding massive power."

"He tried to stop Nuen? And Jasper caught him?" She'd met Jasper. Knew he would not take interference in his affairs well.

Rane laughed. "Not that time. Not the time after that. Soren became obsessed with making Nuen and Jasper pay for what they were doing. We only worked out later that all the powerful sorcerers were doing the same thing. Banishing the wild magic they'd created to the Great Forest."

"So it may not have been Nuen's fault?"

"It didn't matter to Soren. Or to me." He shrugged. "I never had the urge to bring Jasper down, though. I was more interested in reversing the damage. Finding a way to free my father from his enchantment by finding out everything I could about wild magic and how it worked."

"And Jasper caught Soren eventually." She got up on her knees, and Rane rose up, offered her his hand.

"He caught him the night Soren set fire to Nuen's tower. Destroyed all his work." He pulled her to her feet and did not release her hand. "Jasper wants the golden apple badly enough to let Soren go because I think Nuen was hurt in Soren's attack. He must know the apple will heal whoever touches it, as it healed you when you fell from the glass mountain."

"He wants his brother well again, just as you want yours back in one piece." Kayla could understand that. She pulled her hand gently from his grasp.

Rane laughed, and she'd never heard him so bitter. "Nuen is the blunt weapon Jasper uses to grow his power. Without him, Jasper is just another wealthy merchant with a title. If Nuen is injured, Jasper has hidden it, to hide his vulnerability."

"What is going on?" Kayla took the packs Rane held out for her, and slung them over her shoulder. "Eric manipulating my father, Jasper desperate for Nuen to be back at work. More and more strange things in the forest."

"It can only be one thing." Rane rubbed his forehead with stiff fingers. He lifted his head and looked at her, his eyes bleak. "The sorcerers are squaring off. Looking for political allies among the kings, princes and lords. Three years ago almost no-one in the forest had seen wild magic. Now, I doubt there is a single person who hasn't. They are growing their power. Practicing and working large spells, and throwing the wild magic left over into the forest like it's their refuse pit."

She wanted to deny it, but he was right, it could mean only one thing. When she spoke, her voice was small. "They are going to plunge us into a sorcerers' war."

CHAPTER 16

*J*isuel's house stood, rustic and strangely beautiful, in the clearing ahead. The wood and stone building blended naturally into the forest, as entitled to be there as the trees themselves.

Kayla came to a halt, and Rane stood close beside her, feeling the infinitesimal loosening of the enchantment's grip. They stared at the house, neither saying a word.

This was the place. There was no doubting it.

Rane had to wonder why Jisuel had appeared when he had, why he had extended the invitation to them to stay.

Had he somehow learned what Eric had commanded them to do? Or was this the single largest stroke of fortune Rane had ever had?

It could be pure chance, or a trap.

"So Eric did lie. There is no witch called Ylana, he made it up so we wouldn't know we'd have to steal the jewel from Jisuel." Kayla turned, spoke quietly into his ear, and he realized she had the same sense as he, that everything around them was watching. Holding its breath.

"The name Jisuel is enough to give most people pause." He spoke just as quietly back, and drew her closer, looping an arm around her shoulder. He wanted to feel her against him again. She set his senses on fire, but she also calmed him. Helped him find some inner peace.

He would never have thought that would be so, when they had started this journey.

To his surprise, she slipped an arm around his waist and leaned into him, and he brought his other arm up, held her close.

They stood in silence, wrapped together, and Rane felt the tension drain from him. He closed his eyes and breathed her scent.

"Why are people scared of Jisuel? What is he?" Her question was muffled against his shirt.

"No one knows what he is. He buys magical objects, as many from me as he can, and from others. And there are whispers he causes trouble. I've heard it said he's behind the destruction of at least three sorcerers' projects."

"So he has something against sorcerers." Kayla turned her head, rested it against his chest as she looked back at the house. "Which isn't good for us, if we get caught. Given we're working for a sorcerer."

Rane stirred. "Jisuel will hunt us down as soon as he realizes we've taken something from him, no matter who we work for. And he knows this forest better than we do." He noticed wisps of white coming from the chimney, smelled the sweet wood smoke. Somewhere behind them a bird sang a high, trilling song. "We'll have to run. For our lives."

"Unless he already knows what we're planning to do."

Rane nodded. "Yes, I don't discount this is a trap."

She straightened, pulled away from him. "But we're going in there anyway."

He met her eyes, and saw the deep worry etched in them.

"Eric hasn't given us a choice."

"Tell me . . ." She looked away, down to her feet. Lifted her gaze again. "Why did you come to my room the night before the tournament? I would have helped you without . . . what we did together."

His heart stuttered. Something in the way she said it, taking off the armor of her pride, told him she thought they were going to die.

Rane felt the warmth of a sunbeam on his shoulders and neck, heard another bird sing an answer to the first, and faced that possibility himself.

"I had no right." He shrugged helplessly. "I should have walked away, should never have climbed up to your room. When you offered me everything, I meant to say no, to kiss you, and hold you —then leave." He strangled out a laugh. "You caught me in my own game and I forgot why I was even there."

She lowered her eyes, clasped her hands in front of her, her gaze on her twined fingers. "I don't regret it. It gave me strength, sitting up there on that glass mountain, knowing I had defied them all." She smiled, a tight movement that squeezed something in his chest. "You never promised me anything. I thought I'd never see you again. But I won't pretend I wasn't angry and . . . hurt when I realized it was all part of a plan for you."

There was nothing he could say to that that would change things, because he *had* been working a plan. He'd fully intended to walk away with the golden apple and leave her behind, rescuing Soren the only thing on his mind.

Only, it hadn't been. And if Eric hadn't enchanted him, would he have left her?

She watched him, wary, and then turned back to the cottage. He looked at her profile, at her dark hair pulled back at her nape, at the fine wings of her brows over her light gray eyes. And sudden as the flash of a bird breaking cover, he understood.

If Soren's life hadn't been in the balance—if he hadn't needed the golden apple—he would have charged the mountain for her anyway.

"COME IN, COME IN." Jisuel stepped back, waved them inside.

Kayla could not help the little skip of her feet as she hesitated, then forced herself forward.

She felt the solid bulk of Rane behind her, the heat of his body reassuring in the cool, dim interior.

She blinked, her eyes struggling to see anything in the room after the bright light in the clearing outside Jisuel's door.

She closed her eyes to speed the process and Rane's body, pressed against her side, stiffened.

"You are impressed, De'Villier?" Jisuel sounded amused, and Kayla opened her eyes. And gaped.

"Very impressed." There was an edge to Rane's voice, almost pain, and Kayla looked up at him.

His mouth was a thin line, his jaw clenched, and she realized he *was* in pain.

The room they stood in was a quaint kitchen and sitting room, but every available wall space was covered in shelves, and piled onto every one, piled high, were the strange wonders of wild magic. Gems, swords, cups, stones, things she had never seen before, along with the most ordinary household objects.

Rane lifted a hand to his brow, as if to shield his eyes from the sun, and she saw a line of perspiration on his upper lip. He swayed, his face chalky.

"Come outside." She took his arm, led him back to the door.

Jisuel stood in their way.

Rane staggered and she tightened her grip.

"Let me pass. He's too sensitive to these things. There are too many of them in here." She locked gazes with their host, and was overcome again by the strange, hunted feeling she'd had when looking at him in the village.

"Tell me something, first."

Rane tried to shake himself out of his dizziness, and almost pulled her over with him.

"Out of the way!"

Jisuel's eyebrows rose at the sharpness of her tone. "Who are you?"

"Can you not wait until Rane is outside for that?"

She pushed forward, straight at Jisuel, dragging Rane with her, and felt an unpleasant sensation, a prickle against her face, pushing her back.

She jerked, had to clutch Rane to her as her sudden movement almost toppled him.

"Is this how you treat your guests?" She drew herself up, drew on the mantel of princess of Gaynor.

"*Are* you guests?" Jisuel watched her, his eyes narrow, and the feeling that it was so very wrong, that Jisuel himself was wrong, stole over her again.

"Who are *you?*" She breathed the words out, and Jisuel's eyes widened. "You are not what you appear."

"Kayla." Rane ground out her name through clenched teeth. "I am going to—"

Jisuel pulled the door open, and Kayla dragged Rane out. He staggered forward, gasping for breath.

Kayla rested a hand on his bowed back, looked at Jisuel over the top of his head.

He was leaning against the door frame, loose and relaxed.

"I am Kayla of Gaynor."

Jisuel laughed. "A princess? No, you're not."

Kayla cocked her head, and looked at him, long and hard.

He crossed his arms over his chest. Hummed. "Perhaps you are, then. But you are something else, too. That's why I invited you both here."

Kayla lifted a brow.

"Interesting. I'm starting to believe you." Jisuel stepped forward, and Kayla's hand clutched the fabric of Rane's shirt in an involuntary spasm.

"Relax. We have a code of honor in these things."

"We?"

Rane had begun to straighten, his color coming back, and Kayla let her hand slide off him as he rose.

"Witches." Jisuel lifted his arms, and the air around him shivered. Kayla blinked, and in the next instant, standing where Jisuel had been, was a hag.

CHAPTER 17

*a*s Rane straightened, his knife came up. Relief surged through Kayla that he'd recovered so quickly. That he was armed.

The little old lady stood in her doorway as if passing the time of day. "Put that blade away, De'Villier." She sounded like a scolding grandmother.

"Who are you?" Kayla could not take her eyes off the witch. She was tiny, wrinkled, thin. And she exuded power.

"I don't give my name to anyone who asks. But I will give it to another witch. My name is Ylana."

She felt Rane flinch. They'd known it. But standing outside the witch's house, knowing Rane could not enter it—knowing they had to—was a bitter feeling.

"And the Jisuel disguise?" Rane spoke slowly.

"How far do you think I'd have gotten buying magic items like this, eh?" Ylana gestured the length of her body with a hand. "Would you have given me the time of day, De'Villier?"

She snorted, gave him a look that spoke of barely-held contempt. "There would have been more gossip, too. The sorcerers would have heard about an old witch buying wild magic treasures and I didn't want that."

"How do you know I'm a witch?" Kayla stepped forward, ashamed at the pleading in her voice.

Ylana frowned, her face serious. "I do not find that amusing. You know you gave yourself away."

"How? How did I do that?"

Ylana watched her with narrow eyes. "I knew when you threatened me and wild magic gathered at your fingertips." She took a step forward herself. "How do you use wild magic?"

"I don't use it." Kayla stumbled back, sensed Rane right behind her. He had not put away the knife.

"It gathered at your hands. I saw it. I have never known wild magic to do anyone's bidding. How do you command it?"

Kayla shook her head. "I don't know. I don't think I do command it. It has obliged me, a time or two, I'll admit, but I had no say in that."

"Obliged you? Tell me." Ylana's voice was sharp.

"It saved my life twice. Both times from creatures of its own making." She slid a look at Rane, unsure of whether to speak of the window into Eric's dungeon. That would bring them too close to their reason for being here, and she didn't think it a good idea.

Rane gave a tiny shake of his head.

"And yes, when I told you to apologize to Rane, I did feel something. Some power, but I did not call it to me. It just appeared."

Ylana gave a short laugh. "Wild magic doesn't 'just appear'. And I have never known it to oblige anything or anyone. I've lived three hundred years in this forest, and wild magic has always been here."

"Always?" Rane's question was shocked.

"Ah. Not like it is now. Turn a corner and you bump into it, these days. But it isn't a new thing. Where there are powerful spells, there is always wild magic. The old sorcerers had a respect for magic this new breed has forgotten. They did not call too much sky magic down at once unless there was a reason, and that reason was never personal power."

"And the witches, what is their part in this?" Kayla felt a fool for asking, but she knew nothing of witches. Almost too little, she realized now. As if it had been kept from her.

Ylana stared at her. Opened her mouth and closed it again. Turned to the house, and stood just within the doorway. "I am not sure what you are about, Kayla of Gaynor. Either you mock me or there is a mystery here I cannot see. When you are ready to tell me which it is, you are welcome in my home."

She slammed the door in their faces.

"I HAVE TO GO IN." Kayla looked at the door, then back at Rane.

A bird called, just above them, and Rane twisted his head to look up at it. It stared back, and he had the uncomfortable sense of being watched.

"Come." He drew her down the path, and even the immediate press of the enchantment at their retreat was nothing to the thought of her going into the cottage where he could not protect her.

They stopped just out of sight of Ylana's house. He didn't release his hold on her arm, and she did not pull it away. He drew her closer and they stood, touching, the lazy light of afternoon warming them. Kayla's breath was warm on his skin through the cotton of his shirt, and he tightened his hold.

She lifted her face to his. "Eric might have been lying about my being a witch, but Ylana isn't. If things were different, she might help me understand what I am. About what it means to be a witch."

"If things were different." He spoke softly, his lips almost touching her ear. He heard the trace of bitterness in his words, and closed his eyes.

He'd never had time for bitterness, before. He'd tried to change things instead. Soren was the one who'd held a grudge. His brother accepted their father was gone and sought retribution. Rane had never given up hope—he'd pursued knowledge, the key to reversing what had been done.

He didn't know which of them was better off.

He opened his eyes again, pressed a kiss against Kayla's hair. A flash of movement caught his eye. A squirrel was watching them from a branch. It had the same intelligent, focused stare as the robin.

Kayla stirred in his arms. "What—"

He placed a finger on her lips. Nothing they said was safe.

Kayla turned her head and stiffened at the sight of the squirrel. There was a strange crackle in the air. She stepped away from him and faced it.

Rane blinked. The air danced with flickers of purple and green.

"Go." Kayla pointed at the squirrel and it ran, leaping fluid as water through the trees, until it stopped, just in view.

"How do you do that?"

She turned, and he saw the strain on her face. "I don't like being spied on. It was the same when I forced Jisuel to apologize. I think when I'm angry, I can use wild magic."

"I can't go in to the cottage with you and be of any use." Rane watched the squirrel coming back, cautiously moving from tree to tree. "There is too much magic in there, it pulls me in a thousand directions at once."

"I'll do everything I can to find the gem. Eric described what it looked like well enough." Kayla looked over her shoulder and lifted her hands. The squirrel stopped short.

Rane caught her chin. "I'll be as close as I can be. Even if you can't see me." He touched his lips to hers, drew back.

She nodded, set her shoulders and spun in the direction of the cottage. Strode toward it.

The squirrel raced her back.

CHAPTER 18

*K*ayla stood before the door and looked over her shoulder, met Rane's gaze for the last time before he stepped back into the trees. She lifted her hand and knocked.

The door swung open, and as it did she felt the light brush of fingers on her nape, felt the warmth of Rane's invisible body behind hers. A final promise he was just outside. Watching through the windows, through whichever crack he could find.

"Where is De'Villier?" Ylana was suddenly there, half-shadowed in the doorway, and Kayla stiffened.

"Waiting along the path for me. He's too sensitive to your collection." Her voice was breathless.

Ylana stepped back and allowed her entrance.

Rane's hand touched her shoulder and slipped off as she stepped within. Fear rose in her, in tandem with the high-pitched creak of the door shutting.

She was alone.

Rane may be outside, but she was face to face with a woman who could become a man with the lift of her hands, whose power radiated from her in tangible waves, green and brown.

The gloom darkened as the door swung shut, and Kayla smelled the sweet, dusty scent of dried lavender and rosemary, the dark, nutty flavor of burnt butter.

A candle flickered on a rough wooden table, then settled to a steady light as the door clicked shut.

In the half-light, the shelves glowed with their burden of magic trinkets. Some looked ordinary—pedestrian objects she would not have glanced at twice—and others shone with a beautiful light.

Despair draped chains over her shoulders as she took in the sheer number. How would she find Eric's gem in this without Ylana realizing she was looking for something specific?

"Why are you here?" Ylana was watching her, bright and sharp as a robin.

Kayla turned from her and looked down at her hands. "I am here because you invited me."

She had no reason for being in the forest. No possible reason other than the truth. And the truth would doom her. Would doom Rane and his brother, too.

"Don't play games. Why would Kayla of Gaynor come into the Great Forest with a woodsman?"

Kayla lifted her head. There it was. The derisive thread in Ylana's voice. That disrespect for Rane.

She felt the shimmer of anger again. "He may be a woodsman, but he is also my betrothed."

"De'Villier? The future king of Gaynor?" Ylana laughed.

"Why do you think so little of him?"

"I cannot stand his kind. They sell wild magic treasure to the highest bidder. Without a thought to what it could do. Or who they sell it to."

"You want them to only sell to you?" Kayla felt her anger growing.

"Sorcerers shouldn't benefit from wild magic by being offered its treasure. They should be forced to think twice about creating it." The words were hissed, furious.

"Rane is honorable. He doesn't deserve your contempt."

"Yes, he does." Her voice was bitter. "He is hatching a plot. He asks too many questions about wild magic. Finds more treasure than anyone else."

"You saw for yourself, he's sensitive to the objects wild magic creates, he finds them easily. As for asking questions, he has his reasons, and they are nothing to do with you." Kayla reached out a hand and picked up a ring lying on the shelf in front of her. The square-cut gem glinting on the heavy gold band was purple, holding an inner light.

"Don't touch." Ylana's voice was a whip crack, and with a gasp, Kayla let the ring clatter to the floor.

She lifted her gaze to Ylana. "Why are you collecting everything you can? Store-housing all the magic objects of the Forest?"

"Every piece I collect is a piece they cannot have."

Kayla heard the weariness in the witch's voice. Wondered how long Ylana had been racing about as Jisuel, collecting every item she could find.

"It's important the sorcerers don't have these things?" She had to force the question out, for wasn't she there to steal one of Ylana's hard-won treasures for a sorcerer?

"There is something brewing. A clash of sorcerers. They are so powerful now they rub up against each other, irritating each other. Wanting to show each other just how powerful they are. Every piece in my collection would give them some advantage. And at no cost."

"No cost?" She understood so little.

Ylana took a spoon off the table, bent and fumbled under a chair. She straightened, the spoon handle through the band of the ring Kayla had dropped. She carried it like a dead rat back to its shelf.

"Every spell they cast costs something. They are creating magic and its creation comes at a price. It leaches their energy, weakens them. But wild magic has already been created. It already exists, so there is no further price to pay for it. It uses itself up, not the other way around. The cost is nothing but a weakening of the thing itself, until at last it cannot be used again." Ylana watched her as she spoke, and Kayla had the sense she was being measured and weighed.

She took a deep breath. "And the magic you use? There is no price for using that?"

"Earth magic? The sorcerers dismiss earth magic, because it cannot create things not found in nature. But they have forgotten how powerful it is." Ylana smiled. "And they are afraid of it because the price for using it is that the user is bound more tightly to it, is forced deeper and deeper into a guardianship of nature. Something that would not suit them. Not at all. But you should know this."

"I have never used earth magic." She met Ylana's gaze at last.

"You're a witch, even untutored you would have called it without thinking." Ylana lifted her arm and pulled her sleeve up. In the half-light of the room, Kayla had to lean forward to see.

From Ylana's wrist, up past her elbow, was an intricate pattern of leaves and flowers, birds and squirrels, a swirling, entwined rope of fecund nature.

"Pull up your sleeve."

There was nothing there, but Kayla obliged, exposing her inner-wrist. She remembered how Eric had done the same when he'd grabbed her on the stairs in his dungeon.

Now she understood what he had been looking for. His talk of extraordinary control or total ineptitude.

As she pushed up the fine cotton of her sleeve, she wondered whether her father knew the price of earth magic. It might explain why she knew nothing of her heritage. A princess's duty was to the kingdom. There could be no devotion stronger than that. Certainly not the kind of symbiosis Ylana was talking about with earth magic.

Could he have found a way to stop her calling it? A way to deny her nature? And what of her mother? If Eric was right, she had been a witch, too.

Surely an ill-fit with being the queen of Gaynor.

She held out her arm. There were no leaves, no tattoo to mark her use of earth magic, but there was something. She frowned, leaned closer, and Ylana reached out and grabbed her wrist, yanked it to the candle on the table.

There in the yellow light, clear as Ylana's leaves, were three tiny circles.

Ylana pressed down on one circle. "When you drew power to you, to make me apologize." She pressed the other. "And when you chased me off from your tryst with De'Villier, just now. I don't know the third." She released Kayla's arm.

Kayla lifted her wrist closer to her face, rubbed a thumb over the marks. "Chased you?" As she looked up, Ylana's features altered, formed the pointed ears, the sharp features of a squirrel, and in a blink, she was herself again.

"I have never heard of anyone calling wild magic. Or having it answer the call." Ylana reached out for her arm again, but Kayla held it against her chest, her fist clenched.

"Perhaps I didn't know any better."

Ylana let out a surprised laugh. "Perhaps. There is more than a bit of truth in that."

"Is there a way . . . A way my father or mother could have bespelled me so that I did not call earth magic? To keep me from becoming more connected to it than my duty to Gaynor?"

Ylana looked at her in horror. "Who would do such a thing? Which side is your magic from?"

Kayla recalled Eric's words. "My mother, and my father's mother."

"Both sides." Ylana began to move around her, looking at her from all angles. "That is the one thing they couldn't hide. You were too strong, it shines out of you, and they are lucky the wrong people didn't see . . ." She reached out and yanked a hair from Kayla's head. Threw it on the candle's flame. It flared up in a bright green spark.

"Oh, yes. You are bespelled. And if that spell is to prevent you from calling earth magic, it has been done by a witch more powerful than I." She laughed. "Your grandmother, perhaps? But what she didn't take into account was that because you are so strong, you have always been calling magic. Calling it, and calling it, and never having an answer. And when you stepped into the Great Forest you were calling it still."

"And wild magic answered the call."

Ylana laughed again. "It came to you, hungry for a connection."

"I wonder if I can call it now." Kayla held both hands in front of her, flexed her fingers. "How do you call earth magic?"

"You think of it, hidden in everything around you, and you think of what you want to do."

Had she done that when she'd called wild magic before? She remembered her anger, both times she'd called wild magic today. When had she called it a third time?

She suddenly recalled walking along the path, thinking of Rane, of kissing him, of breaking down the walls between them. Recalled how they had fallen into each others arms, the wild magic just behind them. It had embraced her like a lover, afterward. Bathed her in its light, as if delighted to have a companion at last.

Could it be that she had really done that? Broken down the barriers between them?

She blushed. Rubbed her wrist again. "Do witches take lovers?"

Ylana looked startled. "Perhaps, in the beginning. But I've told you, the price of earth magic is being bound to it. It becomes everything, in the end. Family, lover, friend. There is no room for anything else."

She did not think she would be happy in a life that had no room for anything but her calling. "I would not like that."

"There is no like or dislike." Ylana dismissed her words with a wave of her hand. "But your parents have certainly stunted you. Changed you in a way that is contrary to the code." She tapped her lips with tiny, wrinkled fingers. "I will have to change that."

There was something calculating in her eyes, and Kayla had the sense she meant to do what she thought right, whether Kayla agreed with it or not.

With a deep breath she pictured wild magic, the purple green of it, spinning in the air, and then she imagined Ylana, standing beside her kitchen table. Imagined her frozen, her power contained.

She looked at her fingers, and felt a tingle down her spine at the flickers of purple-green light at their tips.

She raised them to show to Ylana, felt a connection to some unlimited supply of power.

"You have called it again," Ylana's voice was excited, wondering, and Kayla felt guilt slam into her, hard as a body blow, and her connection to the magic wavered.

She closed her eyes, and considered her options, but she could see no way around what she planned to do. She opened herself up again.

"Now," she whispered, and wild magic shot from her hands, coalesced around Ylana.

She waited, tensed for a retaliation. Waited for Ylana to break the bonds, to snap free and strike back.

There was silence.

Ylana stared at her, conscious, furious, but absolutely still.

Kayla lifted a beseeching hand. "I am sorry." She turned her arm and saw a fourth circle at the base of her wrist, dark against the luminous white of her skin. She turned to the shelves. "I am here to steal from you."

CHAPTER 19

a whisper of power slithered over the back of Rane's neck, and he spun round, sure he'd find a ball of wild magic behind him.

There was nothing.

And suddenly, from within the cottage, there was silence. The murmur of conversation between Kayla and Ylana had been too soft for him to hear the words, but now there was no sound at all.

Rane turned back to the shutters and pressed himself hard against them, his eye up against the narrow crack. He could see Ylana, still standing by the table, and Kayla, staring at a shelf. Her hand reached out, hesitated, and then grasped whatever it was she had found.

Rane was thrown back, landing hard on the ground.

As he looked up, the roof came off the cottage, an explosion of purple light blowing it straight up.

Rane scrambled to his feet and saw the purple light was encased, contained, by a filigree of purple green. A net of wild magic.

As suddenly as it had erupted, the light cut off, and the roof came down, thatch falling like golden rain all about him.

He ran for the door, his heart stuttering in his chest, but before he could reach it, it slammed open. Kayla stepped out, her hair wild, her eyes huge in her face. There was a small bundle in her hand, held away from her.

"Are you all right?" He wanted to touch her, reassure himself she was safe, but she held up a shaking hand to stop him, looked over her shoulder, and he saw Ylana still standing at the table. With the roof gone, she was bathed in the full light of late afternoon, her face set in a strangely animated expression of fury.

"This is the gem." Kayla lifted the wrapped stone, but did not offer it to him. He reached forward for it anyway and she jerked it back. "Don't touch. Not with your bare hands. I don't know how I . . ." She looked down at her fingers. "I used wild magic instinctively, forced the power up, instead of out." She spoke slowly. "If you had been the one to take it, you'd be dead."

Rane took the rag bundle from her hand, carefully drew aside the corners, and peered at the huge lavender gem within. "Eric doesn't know how dangerous it is, or he'd have warned us." He covered it over again, dropped it carefully into his pouch. "It does him no good if we're dead."

"Perhaps he won't be as fast as I was. Perhaps he'll kill himself with it." She spoke as if detached from herself, still shocked. Then she twisted her arm, lifted it, and he saw a tiny pattern at the base of her wrist, five balls set in an upward spiral.

"What is that?" He caught her hand and drew it toward him, ran a thumb over the pattern, his finger gliding over the velvet smoothness of her skin.

"The wild magic." Her other hand covered his, stilled his fingers. "Every time I call it, it marks me."

He bit back the denial that sprang within him. The thought of the magic branding her was like the scrape of an axe-head across stone, tearing at him.

He slipped his arms around her. Before he could bend his head, take her mouth, she lifted a finger to his lips.

"It has done something else." Her eyes searched his, as if she were unsure how to tell him.

"What?" His whole body tensed. There was no enemy to fight but he could not help the surge of adrenalin that ran through him.

"When I contained the power of the gem, when I sent it through the roof . . ." She looked down at her wrist again. "It broke Eric's enchantment." She looked up with wide eyes. "I'm free."

KAYLA'S FREEDOM was a good thing. A very good thing.

It gave him the first sense of ease he'd had since he'd snatched the golden apple from the air.

Rane lit the pile of wood he'd gathered in Ylana's clearing, and it leapt into flame. He stood, tipped back his head and watched the sky turn from deep indigo to black. The stars were bright, close enough to touch and yet infinitely out of reach. They put him in his place.

His gaze moved lower, rested on Ylana's roof, now as good as new. He hadn't looked, but there would be another circle on Kayla's inner wrist.

"I should release her." Kayla stepped out of the dark, a few logs from Ylana's store under her arms, and followed his gaze to the house.

"You release her, and everything is for nothing." He turned his back on the cottage, and sank down on his haunches beside the fire. "Do not expect her to understand why we did it."

"I think you may find that she would understand. That she could be a great help to us."

Rane lifted his head. "I know her. Dealt with her for years. She won't forgive me for this, no matter what she thinks of you. Please don't do it. Soren's life is at stake and I don't want to risk it."

"All right." There was a heaviness to her response, and she set the logs down carefully, crouched beside him. "I don't know if she feels hunger, or stiffness, the way I've left her. I do know she is very angry."

"Yes." There was nothing more to say. They could not release the witch. Not without risk of their lives. He truly believed that.

"We are forced to steal for Eric. To give him something he

should not have. That he will use against us when he has it." Kayla knelt closer to the fire, lifted her hands to its warmth. "I've been forced to enchant someone as he enchanted us. Forced to go against everything I believe is right."

She looked fierce, strong. Beautiful. The flames behind her leapt as high and hot as his desire and he reached across and took her hands. "We'll find a way to bring Eric down."

The light of the fire caught her gray eyes, and they flashed silver. She drew their entwined hands to her lips, kissed his knuckles. Her hair fell as she bent her head, brushing his arms and making him shiver. "We must rescue Soren first. We can't do anything until he is safe."

The way she spoke, as if there was no question they would do it together, made it impossible for him to reply. He drew her to him.

The kiss he gave her was slow and gentle. The kind of kiss a man gives his lover when they have no hurry, nothing pressing to do but lie with each other and explore. He shut out the enchantment, the pounding need to run. Shut out everything but her.

He lifted her so she straddled his lap, ran his hands from her shoulders up her throat and buried them deep in her hair. He put his lips to her neck, just below her ear and breathed deep.

When he pulled back, she was watching him, eyes glittering in the firelight.

She said nothing, her hands going down to the hem of her shirt. As she lifted it over her head, as he slid trembling hands over her, he knew there was only one thing he could do, now she was free of the enchantment. Only one way to keep her safe and protect her as he had not been able to do until now.

Face Eric alone.

CHAPTER 20

*K*ayla woke up cold.

Struggling with her blanket, she rose on an elbow and pushed her hair out of her eyes. Looked around the clearing.

Rane was gone.

She had a stomach-dropping feeling he wasn't getting wood, or fetching water from the stream that ran behind Ylana's cottage. The silence was too perfect.

He had left her.

She rose to a crouch, and saw a large, flat river stone propped against her saddlebag. He'd written on it with a piece of charcoal from the fire.

Stay hidden. Wait for me.

Since the start of their journey, he'd protected her. Put his life in danger for her. She should not be surprised he'd done it again.

But she was. Surprised and hurt. And angry.

No, *furious*.

She wondered when he'd made his decision. While they crouched together by the fire, while he kissed her, while they rocked and thrust, limbs entwined, naked in the flickering flame-light?

Even though she knew he wanted her safe, she felt betrayed. They had been a team. That's what she'd thought. He would never have got the gem without her. She would never have made it to Ylana's without him.

She pushed the stone aside, dug into her pack, and her fingers closed around the smooth, cool surface of the golden apple. A prickle ran up her fingers and she let it go.

He had left it with her.

It mollified her, a little. She'd believed he would come back, but the apple was proof.

She closed her bag, her skin still tingling, and stood. Looked at Ylana's cottage.

Did she dare release the witch now Rane was gone? And if Ylana, with her three hundred years' experience, got the better of her? And took the apple?

She couldn't risk it. Her eyes slid away from the house, her stomach fluttering and her skin clammy with guilt and self-recrimination. She turned away, back to the camp, and wondered what to do next.

She felt cut adrift, with no enchantment clinging to her, directing her feet and her thoughts. And she felt gloriously free.

There was a faint snap of a twig, just in front of her and she stilled. The leaves of a bush rustled.

She looked around for a weapon, and then remembered she had one at her fingertips.

Waited . . . waited.

A black streak of muscle and fur leapt, and she raised her hands, the air dancing purple and green, before she realized who it was.

"Sooty."

The cat raced around her, mad with glee, kittenish on a terrifying scale. Then she rolled on her back, and Kayla knelt beside her, rubbed her under her chin.

Her familiar.

She grinned. Felt a stir of excitement deep in her stomach.

She was no witch, and no worthy princess of Gaynor, if she hid in the forest for Rane to come for her.

As the purrs of contentment rumbled through the clearing, Kayla thought through her options.

Follow Rane. But she had no idea when he'd started out, no idea where Eric lived. No enchantment to force her in the right direction.

She did know the way to Therston, though, through the village where they'd met Jisuel. And she knew who was in need of help in Therston.

Soren De'Villier.

RANE RAN. And with every step the forest held him back. Brambles clutched at his clothes, branches blocked his path. Sweat glistened on his chest and face, and his shirt stuck uncomfortably to his back, though the sun had yet to break free of the horizon.

His breathing sounded loud and rasping to his ears, his footsteps clumsy.

The paths he'd taken with Kayla seemed suspiciously wide and clear, now, as if their way had been smoothed. He should have wondered at that before—he was used to traversing the narrow, choked tracks of the forest—but the enchantment, and the woman in front of him, had somehow made him forget the Great Forest was never usually so accommodating.

He remembered now, though.

He leapt a log and landed on a floor packed tight with dry sticks and dead leaves. His every step crunched as though he ran across a river of beetles.

The enchantment was rewarding him for his efforts, lifting its hold, allowing him to move without the choking feeling of panic.

But he wasn't running to accommodate Eric's spell. He'd left Kayla alone. Without protection. Whatever happened with Eric, he wanted to get it done. Get back to her.

Last night it seemed better to leave Kayla than put her in Eric's reach. He'd seen the look in Eric's eyes when he'd watched her at

Gaynor Castle and Rane wasn't prepared to make it easy for Eric to get what he wanted. To get what was Rane's.

Because she was his now. When they started the journey, no matter his legal rights, she had not been.

Last night they had given themselves to each other and he was as much hers as she was his.

His breathing settled into a steady rhythm as he ran. He twisted and leapt over the obstacles in his way, his arms scratched and bleeding as he threw branches aside to keep up his pace.

He was going so fast, he smelled the smoke too late. He broke into the clearing, into their midst, before he could stop, surprising them as much as himself.

One of the men gave a shout, and they jumped to their feet.

Rane had jerked back, but he threw himself forward as soon as he realized who they were, leaping their camp-fire and heading straight for the path on the other side of the clearing.

Someone leapt at him from the right and he put on a spurt of speed. Arms locked around his legs and he hit the ground, kicking out.

"No, you don't."

Someone sat on his back, and hands dealt roughly with his legs, tying them with rope. His arms were yanked back as well, and when they were tied too, he was flipped over.

"De'Villier." It was Travis, his old companion from his time in Jasper's service, and Rane nodded to him, his expression blank.

"Jasper is looking for you."

Rane nodded again. "I know."

"Why haven't you brought him what he wants, or do you not care if your brother dies?" Travis sat down on a log pulled up for a seat next to the fire, and Rane saw there were four other men. He did not know them. They watched him attentively.

A search party sent out to find him.

"I care. Eric had an enchantment on that apple. I have to do something for him first, only then will the apple be mine to give to Jasper."

Travis looked at him, his eyebrows raised. "Eric is making you do something for him first?"

Rane grimaced. Even this small delay pressed the heel of the enchantment harder against his throat. When he spoke, it was through clenched teeth. "The contest was a trap. A way to find someone with the ability to get the apple. When I touched it, it enchanted me."

"Well, Eric will have to wait. I'm to bring you to Jasper." Travis stood and Rane's heart jumped in panic.

He took a deep breath. "Let me go, Travis."

Travis shrugged, the movement one of genuine regret. "Sorry. Jasper said to find you and bring you to him."

"It will be worse for Jasper if you take me to him. I swear it."

Travis moved from his log, crouched beside him. "I cannot let you go."

Rane felt another wave of panic. Just hearing the words seem to trigger the enchantment into a flurry of punishments. Heart beating harder, breathing kicking up.

"I'm sorry." Travis' hand reached for Rane's belt, undid his pouch. Tipped it out. Rane turned his head, looked at the small pile of coins, his black firestick and the moonstone lying in an unassuming heap. Travis grunted, frowning, and scooped them back into the leather purse. His eyes went to Rane's knife sheath. He unbuckled it, pulled out the knife.

As usual, it looked blunt. Useless.

It was the reason Rane had not sold it when he'd found it, right at the beginning, when he'd still thought the best things were the most beautiful, the shiniest. He knew better now.

As it was he'd only discovered its unusual properties by mistake. And he had never considered selling it after that.

"Huh." Travis slammed it back into its sheath and threw it down next to the pouch. He narrowed his eyes. "You don't have the golden apple?"

Rane shook his head. He thought of the gem, tightly wrapped in a soft cloth, strapped around his waist under his clothes, and hoped Travis would not physically search him.

"How is Soren?" He spoke quietly, but Travis reacted as if he'd shouted in his ear, flinching away from him.

"He's alive."

The way he said it gave Rane no comfort.

He was shivering, he realized. His muscles pulsing against the ropes, sending pain shooting through his arms and legs.

"What is happening to him?" One of the men moved, stood beside Travis.

"Enchantment." Rane got the words out through chattering teeth, although he was not cold. It was as if his body was trying to shake its way along the path.

"Do you know what became of Djan?" One of the others asked, kneeling beside Travis.

Rane tried to keep his body still. "Wild magic got him, and his companion."

"Got him?"

Rane didn't answer. They should know what happened in the forest, and if they didn't, they would soon learn.

He wondered what they would have done if Kayla had been with him. Studying the harsh features and scars of the motley group, he was glad he had left her behind.

"Let's go." Travis gave a flick of his hand, and each of the four men took a shoulder or a leg, lifted Rane up high, face down.

He saw Travis's feet start ahead, stop and turn back to the camp. Heard the chink of coins in his pouch as they were lifted.

Travis passed them again, and Rane twisted his neck to see if his knife was with the pouch. It was. Clutched loosely in Travis' hand.

"Travis. Let me go. Before it's too late."

"I said, let's go," Travis called from up ahead.

The men began to move, and with every step, took Rane closer to madness.

CHAPTER 21

*I*t hardly took them any time to reach the village. Kayla thought the forest seemed lighter today—the paths wider, the sun shining through the trees and reaching all the way to the forest floor.

She was sure the way had been longer and harder yesterday.

As she and Sooty stepped out onto the green, the cows began lowing, the pathetic, desperate sounds of creatures in terror, and Kayla saw Sooty crouch down, her front paws massaging the ground, her back legs quivering.

"Sooty."

The cat froze in surprise at the sharpness of her tone, turned its head to her.

"No chasing cows. Come here."

The cat blinked. Her tail flicked in anger.

She was a cat, not a dog, Kayla remembered. Not prone to obedience. And Sooty had been wild for more than a few weeks.

She could try magic, but she was reluctant to command the cat that way. It would be better to be obeyed without it. She stared the cat down.

"Come here." Her voice was gentle this time, coaxing.

Sooty rose from her crouch, sat, and looked the other way. Her tail flicked again.

Kayla grinned.

"Let's go." She took a few steps across the green, turned and waited for the cat, and eventually, with great disdain, Sooty joined her, moving to her side and then rubbing her cheek against Kayla's thigh, marking her.

"You can't bring that cat here." It was Gert, calling from the bottom step of his house.

"She will stay with me." Kayla shielded her eyes against the sun, just behind his roof.

"She's a cat. She goes where she likes. Frightens the cows."

"We are taking the path to Therston, we will be gone in a moment." Kayla kept her eyes on Gert, but she continued on across the field, her hand sinking into Sooty's fur.

"Where is the troll-killer?" Gert stepped out from the shade of his house, and Kayla saw he had his axe in hand.

"We had to go our separate ways for a time." They had reached the path, and Kayla relaxed a little. Sooty had stayed with her, for once unconcerned with peripheral movement.

"Why does that cat mind you?" Gert took another step toward them, and Kayla could hear the tight suspicion in his voice.

"She is a creature of wild magic. And wild magic is . . . sympathetic to me."

"Sooty!" A tiny figure darted from Gert's door, brown hair flying back, little knees lifting. A small girl with hair in braids leapt from the porch to the ground, red dress streaming out behind her. "Sooty!"

"Marie, no." Gert's cry was strangled, and he lunged at the child, missing her and stumbling forward.

Sooty turned at the sound, and Kayla could feel her vibrate with excitement.

"Sooty." It was a warning, but it wasn't enough. Sooty bounded toward the child.

"She's not your kitten any more." Gert righted himself and ran forward, hand outstretched to grab his daughter.

Sooty dodged right, then left, in a wild kitten game, her paw out to bat at her tiny former owner in a playful swat.

"Stop." Kayla threw her hands forward. She did not wait to see if wild magic had gathered at her fingers, she trusted it would be there. She needed it to be there.

And it was.

Sooty froze, mid-leap. Her back paws on the ground, her front paws above the little girl's head. The sparkle of wild magic glinted off her fur.

Gert snatched his daughter up and put her behind him, raised his axe.

"No!" Kayla's hands flashed again, and Gert stood as still as the cat he was about to kill.

Marie stood, opened-mouthed, and a woman Kayla had not noticed came behind the child and lifted her into her arms. Turned her face away from the scene and pressed it into the curve of her neck.

"I know Sooty has caused you trouble, but she didn't mean harm. This is her home and she hasn't realized that she is too big. She doesn't understand." Kayla reached the two statues. "I will take her with me, and give her a home. Your husband has no need to kill her."

The woman nodded, her eyes steady, even though Kayla could see her hands trembled where they stroked her daughter's back. "You'll release him?"

Kayla looked at the way the cat and the man were set in place. If she released Gert, he could still kill Sooty as he came free. She turned and saw where the path disappeared into the forest toward Therston, and lifted her hands. Sooty was suddenly there, still frozen, waiting for Kayla to join her.

Kayla began walking backward, and when she was out of Gert's range, her hands flashed, and the woodsman fell forward, axe spinning through the air to land on the green.

"What are you?" He bent, hands on knees, panting.

Kayla looked down at her hands. They were still tingling. "It seems I am a wild magic witch."

RANE HAD LOST all sense of time and place.

His agitation had given way to gibbering and then to silent shivering.

Sometimes he would moan, hearing himself as if he were apart, locked in a cold, lonely chamber, while the enchantment held the rest of the castle. Of him.

He hung between the men, dizzy, desperate. Helpless.

He didn't know for how long.

And then slowly, like the first taste of sweet water after a hike through the desert, the enchantment eased a little. It lifted off him, inch by inch.

He was aware of a change in the light, of the movement of air around him, and forced his eyes open. They had reached the edge of the forest. Rane sensed a lift in the men's spirits.

He could only think they had, by chance, swung in the direction of Eric's castle, had eased his burden, however minutely.

He needed to escape. A sense of urgency pounded at him, intensifying as he came back to his senses.

They had stopped walking, and Rane saw they'd entered a clearing. It held the rough remains of an old camp, an abandoned horse-cart to one side.

He jerked against his captors.

"Watch it." The man at his left shoulder smacked his head, and he thrashed, throwing his body from side to side, twisting against the hold they had on him.

"That's enough." Travis's tone was hard. Harder than Rane had ever heard it.

"Can't help it," he muttered. "Enchantment." He twisted again.

Travis hit him. A swift, clipped blow to the forehead, and the world spun for a moment.

No! If he went under now, they could take him to Jasper and he might never wake. Or if he did, he would be insane.

"Please." He lifted a hand.

Travis hit him again.

He could not let it end here.

He fought, flailing and bucking, catching the men by surprise. He was free for a moment, his heart leaping as he fell, and then he hit the ground, losing the air in his lungs, rolling until he stopped suddenly against a fallen log.

He groaned, curling inward.

"He's got something under his shirt." One of the men crouched beside him, yanked the shirt higher. Exposed the strip of cloth around his waist, and the small lump where he'd strapped the gem to the small of his back.

"Don't touch . . ." His teeth were chattering, and he clamped them together, spoke through a clenched jaw. "Don't touch it."

Travis ignored him, taking the small wrapped bundle and crouching down. His men joined him in a loose circle, and Travis flicked the cloth open.

He was going to touch it. Of course he was.

Grunting with effort, Rane lifted up, leaned on the log, flipped himself over it to the other side. It was not a lot of cover, but it was better than nothing.

He pressed himself into the wedge between the ground and log, and winced as there was a sudden flash of purple.

Only one man screamed. The rest never got the chance.

There was nothing more.

Rane waited one minute. Then another.

He lifted his head up and looked over the top of the log.

He was alone.

The gem lay, winking and glittering in the oblique light of the sun, nestled amongst the packs and bags the men had dropped when they'd crouched together.

Rane wondered if they were dead. Or changed.

There were no frogs on the ground this time.

He struggled up onto the log, swung his legs over and slid off it onto his backside. Shuffled himself forward, until he reached the place Travis had knelt and thrown down his things.

He tipped everything out of Travis' pack, and by the time he had his knife wedged between his tied hands, he was sweating with effort, his body shaking as the enchantment throttled him.

He eased it out of its sheath. Carefully, so carefully, he felt for the dragon, brushed his thumb over it and touched the blade to his ropes. They fell away immediately.

He dropped the knife, rubbing his wrists and biting back a cry of pain as the blood rushed to his hands. The knife lay at his feet, dull, rusted. Nothing.

He smiled as he picked it up again, rubbed his thumb over the dragon cast in relief on the hilt. The blade gleamed a sudden blue, and he bent to the ropes at his feet. As they fell to the ground, he rose up, faced west. The sun had already sunk past the top of the trees, and the sky was aglow with color.

He wondered what hell Soren was living in right now. The thought was bitter on his tongue, because he could do nothing about it, could not take a step in his brother's direction without the enchantment's punishments.

Then he turned back to the camp, carefully wrapped the gem and strapped it to his body. He rifled through Tavis's supplies as fast as he could.

His coin purse was gone. And his moonstone with it. Travis must have attached it to his own belt.

He closed his eyes and clenched his fists against the flash of anger and loss at the moonstone, but there was nothing he could do. No way to get it back.

He took all the food he could carry, two water bottles, and found a path north east. Began to run.

With every step, the enchantment eased the hold on his throat a little more, and a new weight rested heavier on his shoulders.

Because knowing what it could do, he could not give the gem to Eric.

CHAPTER 22

*D*arkness fell like a wave from behind, eating up the forest, while in front of Kayla, due west, the sky was bright gold.

Wild magic had followed them all day as they walked, first one sphere, then another, then another. They dodged and hid behind trees, shot forward and then spun, still and unmoving in mid-air. She did not know how many were around her now, a flock of explosive magic, shimmering purple in the dusk light.

Sooty ignored them.

Kayla had expected to reach a town by now, or have found some sign she was in Therston, but she hadn't seen another person since they'd left the village.

She needed to find a place to camp, but her feet kept moving even though she'd passed more than one suitable clearing.

Rane thought Soren was being tortured, and while he was in Jasper's power, she could not rest.

Without any warning, Sooty stopped on the path, her ears twisting, her nose lifting. She started forward again, half-crouched, and a frisson of fear brushed up Kayla's arms. Her heart beat faster, and she saw her hands were already glowing purple-green in readiness.

The wild magic spheres drew nearer.

She moved forward cautiously, and stepped into a wide clearing. Sooty bounded across to a cart standing to one side, sniffing the corners. There were a few logs placed around an old fireplace, and bags lying on the ground. Abandoned in haste.

Kayla's gaze swept the camp, nervous and ready to flee, but there was no one there.

The night had finally caught up with them, and the sky was in its last deep indigo before it turned black. Here and there, she saw the flicker of wild magic between the trees.

She crouched beside the bags. They were travel packs—full of food, water, clothing and blankets for the road.

Rane had left her more than half the food, but if she rescued Soren, he would need as much as he could get. Clothes, too.

She had a deep sense of unease about this place, as if the people in it had been swallowed up by a dark nothingness.

They weren't coming back.

Her fingers brushed rope, and she lifted up a piece of it, knotted on one side, cut straight and clean on the other. There had been a captive here.

She shivered. Whoever these people had been, they would not miss their supplies.

Sooty sniffed at a log to one side, pawing it a few times. Her ears moved ceaselessly, her body tense. As uneasy here as Kayla.

When Kayla had taken what she could carry from the bags, she hefted her saddle pack over her shoulder.

"Let's go." She was vibrating with an urgency to be gone, her movements jerky.

Sooty looked across at her, then west, and a low growl rumbled from deep in her chest. Fear pricked down Kayla's spine at the sound.

She forced herself to move, crouched down beside the cat. "What it is?"

She heard the voice a moment later, a man calling out.

Another voice responded, and someone stepped into the clearing.

"They aren't here. They'd have come all the way to the strong-hold if they'd gotten this far. Wait . . ." The stranger saw the bags and then Sooty and her almost at the same time, and jerked back.

Sooty growled again, long, low and ending in a hiss.

The second man joined him. a knife in his hand.

"Good evening." Kayla rose from her crouch and inclined her head. Behind the men, on the path they'd used, two spheres of wild magic rose up. "Can you tell me the way to Jasper of Therston?" Her fingers threaded themselves through the raised fur on Sooty's neck.

"What do you want with Jasper?" The first man leaned forward, peering at her in gloom.

"Private business." She flicked back her hair. "You know the way?"

"Aye, we know the way." The second man stepped forward, staring at her boldly. He smiled. "Come with us and we'll take you there."

"Thank you." She did not feel afraid any more. The sight of the spheres steadied her. Made her remember she was not help-less, even though she suspected they meant to do her harm. They did not realize wild magic hovered at their backs, latent with menace.

She put her hands behind her, lest they betray her with a glimmer of light. "Come, Sooty."

Sooty rose to her full height and walked beside her toward the men, still growling faintly at the back of her throat. It occurred to Kayla the men had not realized the size of her before. She was as black as the night, and hard to distinguish from the shadows.

She saw their cocky anticipation turn to fear.

The first man said nothing. He spun back the way they'd come and ran, letting out a shriek at the sight of the wild magic. He ran around it, and it let him pass. The second stumbled back a few steps. "No harm meant." His voice rose high. He spun back to the path and followed his companion, moaning as he passed the wild magic.

They were the first people she'd seen since leaving the village, and the way they'd said Jasper's name made her think they knew him.

Perhaps they were his men.

She rubbed Sooty under the chin, her fingers sparkling with excitement. "Let's follow them."

JASPER WAS a man with something to hide. Or something to protect. His stronghold was worthy of the name, a strange mix of fort and old castle.

As the big gates swung closed on the two men, Kayla moved back between the trees, her heart sinking. At least ten men had stood up on the ramparts, bows lifted, as the running men approached. She would need to find another way in, the front was too well-guarded.

Behind her, the string of wild magic spread out. When one spun close, her hands sparkled bright and hot. It calmed her. Helped her to think.

She pushed up her sleeve. New spheres from her spells this morning on Sooty and Gert spiralled up her inner arm like a stream of bubbles twisting through the water.

Sooty butted her hip and she dropped her sleeve back in place. Time was wasting.

She kept moving, working her way through the dense under-growth until she was behind the compound. It was right at the edge of the forest, and Jasper had had all greenery beaten back at least twenty feet from the fence. To get to it, she would have to step into the open.

The ramparts were empty here. Silent.

She could create a diversion, but she did not want anyone to suspect trouble. She would rather sneak in undetected. And out the same way.

She slid her pack under a bush, taking only the golden apple. If Soren was badly injured, she would need it to heal him. She jammed it into her trouser pocket, felt the weight of it pulling at her belt.

"I want you to stay, puss." Kayla rubbed the cat between her ears. "You'll be hard to hide."

Sooty lifted her head, and Kayla scratched her under her chin. "Stay. Wait for me here."

She lay on the ground and crawled forward, using her hips, elbows and feet. It felt as if she was exposed for minutes, the muscles in her back tensing, expecting the sharp pain of an arrow at any moment.

But nothing.

No alarm sounded, and at last she reached the rough wood of the perimeter fence. She leaned against it, trapping her hands between her body and the wall, and thought of a narrow opening, just wide enough for her to crawl through.

It was harder than it had been before, and she realized she was just outside of the forest here, that using wild magic was an effort.

She wriggled her way back to the treeline, and approached one of the spheres, and a part of it separated, came to her, and she cradled it in her hands for a moment, before putting it in her other pocket.

By the time she had crawled back to the fence again, she was sweating.

She thought again of a small opening, one hand in her pocket, and the flare was muted, light leaking from either side of her body, and there was suddenly an opening where her feet pressed against the fence.

She knelt, stuck her head through, and checked there was no one waiting for her on the other side.

After a beat, she lowered herself to the ground and wiggled through, rose to a crouch in the darkness.

She was in.

Her elation was tempered by the utter silence. It unnerved her. She would prefer to hear some noise in the distance—the quiet made her imagine a thousand eyes on her.

In front of her, a high, long building ran close to the fence, stone walls rising three floors. She looked back and up, saw a wooden platform ran the length of the fence she'd just come through, high enough to bring a man shoulder-height with the top. Wooden ladders were propped against it for access. There were no guards standing watch or walking the boards, there was nothing but a strong stench of burnt wood and tar.

She crept forward and pressed up against the building, felt the rough crumble of sandstone against her fingers.

The feeling of eyes on her was still strong. She moved, quick as she dared, along the wall until she reached the end of the building. Steeled herself to look around the corner.

She hesitated.

It didn't make sense for Jasper to place fewer guards at the back than the front—coming in had been too easy. And the deep, unnatural silence made her so nervous her fingers sparked. She slipped them into her pockets, her left hand tingling in its little sphere of wild magic, her right hand pressed hard against the golden apple.

It saved her.

A bolt, shot from above, from the guards' walk of the stockade wall, slammed into her from behind.

She felt the blow, the pain as it pierced her, and the immediate counter of the apple, her body torn and mended in a moment.

The bolt dropped from her shoulder to her feet, and she tried to run, stumbling, her legs weak, her heart pounding so loud she was deafened by it. Her fingers gripped the apple, and with every step, she felt a new surge of energy.

"You missed!"

The words were shrieked from somewhere above her head. There was a thud and someone cried out.

Kayla ducked around the corner of the building, crouching low. Her breath came in pants. They had been there all along. Some spell had been at work to stop her seeing them.

Men were running toward her across a large open space from the main gate, these ones visible, but she had the sense none saw her, and to make sure they did not, she wished herself invisible. A glow escaped her pocket, but so quick, and so close to the ground, the men who glanced her way did not break their stride. She had the feeling the wild magic she'd brought with her had just used itself up.

She smelled sawdust, and guessed she was facing a training area for Jasper's knights. On the far side stood the castle tower she'd seen from the forest, at the center of the stronghold. She stood and ran, straight into the open, forcing herself to trust her spell would keep her unseen.

She heard the thunder of invisible boots on wood, saw the glow of torches being lit with invisible hands all along the guards' walk. With every step she steeled herself for her own magic to fail, for someone to see her and raise the cry. To notice the soft sand and wood shavings she threw up as she sprinted.

At last she was in the deep shadows of the tower. It stank of smoke. Her fingers came away from its wall gritty with soot. The whole tower had been burned.

She remembered what Rane had told her. This was Soren's handiwork.

A shout rang out, and men turned the corner, running back across the training ring. They spread out and slowed as they found nothing.

"Look for blood," one called out. "There was a hit."

Kayla clutched the apple more tightly, her pulse jumping at the sight of so many men intent on finding her. Intent on doing her harm.

She felt like a princess, suddenly, not a witch. Certainly not a hero.

But Soren De'Villier was already in harm's way. And he had no one else until Rane had faced an even bigger threat than Jasper. And if Rane could take on Eric alone, she could handle this. She had to.

She stayed close to the tower wall and moved fast as she could away from them, following the tower's circular base.

The entrance to the stronghold loomed ahead, huge gates secure. To her left, another large building rose up, and she guessed it was Jasper's main residence. It had a more refined look than the rest of the stronghold, the double doors made of carved wood and some of the windows elegantly arched.

A cobbled drive led up to it.

"There is no one here!" The shout was almost in her ear, and Kayla dropped to the floor, her legs collapsing under her in shock.

A man shimmered into visibility, an elbow's nudge away, his head turned over his shoulder.

Another man appeared a little way away and walked over to join him.

Biting back a whimper, Kayla saw it was Jasper himself, and she lifted up into a crouch.

"What do you think happened to him?" Jasper's voice was edged with fear, and his hands clenched and unclenched on his belt.

The man who'd shouted said nothing, and a look passed between them.

Up on the guards' walk, there were suddenly twenty men, but one made for the nearest ladder, his movements labored. "Did you find her?" His voice was hoarse, querulous.

"Her?" Jasper looked up, his body tense. "I thought it was De'Villier." He spoke as if to a child.

"It was a woman." There was a snap of temper in the statement. "I saw her for a brief moment before she was hit . . ." The man reached the top of the ladder and in the orange glow of the torch-light, Kayla could see more than half his face was burnt and twisted. His shoulder twitched in an uncontrolled spasm.

There was a silence between Jasper and his man.

"Did you see a woman?" Jasper asked eventually, his voice low.

His lieutenant shook his head. "I saw a shadow moving, I'll give him that. Whether it was a man, a woman, or something strange from that god-forsaken forest, I don't know. The two men who went to find Travis said they met a woman and a monster in the forest. It might be her."

"Stop whispering. I'm injured, not stupid." The man swung down onto the ladder, his body jerking with each painful step.

"Keep looking for someone, or something. No sleeping on duty tonight." Jasper spoke fast, to get in everything before the man reached the ground. "I'll take my brother inside. And if it *is* De'Villier, for heaven sake don't kill him. We need him alive."

His lieutenant lifted his hand in salute.

Jasper started forward, broke his stride and turned. "Check Soren. If it *was* De'Villier, that's the first place he'll head."

The man nodded, and stepped back onto Kayla's foot, then spun on his heel, grinding her toes into the ground. He frowned, looked down to see what he was standing on.

Kayla bit her hand to stop herself crying out, refusing to even breathe.

The man continued on, and Kayla hopped her first few steps after him until she got her fingers in her pocket for the apple to do its work.

She would have taken the crushed toes, apple or no, because at last, someone was leading her to what she'd come for.

It was time to stop being a princess.

CHAPTER 23

*W*ater dripped from the green slime coating the ceiling and echoed strangely in the passage. It drowned out any noise Kayla made as she followed Jasper's man ever downward and she was grateful for it.

He walked fast, forcing her to skip around puddles slippery with fungus and lengthen her stride to stay within sight of his torchlight.

Whatever damage the fire had done to the above-ground part of the tower, the tunnel under it was untouched. The walls were streaked bright green, orange and purple with lichen, and the air was heavy with the musty smell of stale water and spores.

The passage twisted in a wide spiral. Jasper's man slowed at the turn ahead, and Kayla heard a sound, a creak of hinges and the squeak of metal rubbing metal.

He lifted the torch higher, and Kayla trailed after him, keeping close to the wall and as far back into the darkness as she could.

They came suddenly and without warning into a large room, rough enough to be a natural cave.

As she stepped into the chamber, Kayla felt a strange sense of being stripped, as if she'd lost something. Her hand went to the apple, but it was in her pocket, and still she could not shake the feeling that something had been taken from her.

There was another clink of metal, and Jasper's man strode forward, torch high.

A man hung from chains by his arms on the far wall, only just reaching the ground with the balls of his bare feet. His face was drawn, hollow, the skin tight around his eyes. His unkempt beard highlighted the stark relief of his cheekbones.

Kayla realized Jasper had narrowed Soren's life to a choice between excruciating pain in his arms and shoulders, or his feet.

"Finally remembered to feed me, did you?" His voice was hoarse, cracked, and he did not look up. His features were a knife stab to her gut. So like Rane, but so gaunt, so beaten down, she could barely look at him.

"No. Just checking up on you."

"Haven't gone anywhere." He wracked out a cough, and Kayla realized he was trying to laugh.

"When last was someone down here?" Jasper's man moved the torch closer to Soren, peering at him.

"Can't remember." It came out as a whisper.

The man cursed under his breath, jamming the torch into a stand in the center of the room. A bucket with a cup hooked to the rim stood next to it, and he scooped out some water, and walked over to Soren.

As the cup touched his lips, Soren lifted his head, his eyes dark in his pale face. He swallowed, his throat working as if he were trying to deal with a piece of steak rather than a few sips of water.

"Your friend is quiet," he said, looking straight at Kayla.

She froze, her heart jumping in shock. How could he see her? She looked down, stared in horror at her hands. How could she see them? As she leapt for the safety of the shadows, her own shadow stretched, then shrank against the cave wall.

"Friend?" The man turned, looking toward the entrance, and Kayla kept very still. After a moment, he turned back to Soren. "What friend?"

"Thought I saw . . ." Soren shook his head as if to clear it, then moved forward eagerly for another sip of water.

He gulped it down, but when he lifted his eyes, he searched for her, his gaze moving from the wall where he'd seen her shadow to the corners of the room.

She recalled the sense of loss as she'd come into the room, wondered if Nuen had cast a spell across the entrance, blocking her ability to call magic.

That she'd felt it, felt naked without it, made her go still inside. The wild magic was already becoming part of her. Unconsciously, her fingers went to her wrist, stroked up her inner arm.

"I'll send down some food. Jasper needs you alive." The man hooked the cup back on the rim of the bucket. Lifted the torch.

Soren's eyes glittered as the flames leapt, his gaze fixed on the light.

She saw he wanted to plead with the man to leave it behind. To not leave him in darkness. His mouth worked, but he would not allow the words out.

Jasper's man walked toward the passageway, then hesitated. She felt a shiver of unease as he did a last survey of the room, his gaze sliding over her. He turned and walked out without another word. Without a backward glance. The light faded, then winked out.

Kayla waited while the sound of his footsteps became faint, then waited a few minutes more. She could take no chances. There had been something about the way his eyes skipped over the corner where she'd crouched that made her heart beat hard and quick.

"Are you going to kill me?" The whisper was hoarse, eerie, in the darkness. "Whoever you are?"

She stood. "I'm here to get you out, not harm you." With total darkness pressing all around, even her whisper sounded loud. She lifted her hands, wished for a light. Then swore as none appeared.

She'd forgotten there was an enchantment on this cave.

"Are you a woman?" He sounded disbelieving.

"Kayla of Gaynor." She took a tentative step forward, wondered how Soren was still sane being kept in utter darkness.

"Kayla of Gaynor." He spoke her name as if in a dream. "I have gone mad." He rattled his chains and let out a cry of anguish. "I have fought it, but it has finally won."

Kayla stumbled across to him, hands in front of her, and touched his shoulder. Curled her fingers around his upper arm.

He went still, his whole body tense.

"I am not here to harm you, I swear." Kayla fumbled in her pocket for the apple, wondered if Nuen's enchantment would affect it. It seemed to her intrinsically magical, older than the sky, and the earth and the wild magic Ylana had told her about.

She lifted it up. "Rane—"

"What do you know of Rane?" Soren's voice echoed harsh and over-loud in the chamber. Under her fingers, his muscles were hard as iron.

"I know . . ." Kayla trailed off. Anything she said about Rane would give her away. She had no wish to expose herself, in the dark, in this strangely intimate position, to a stranger.

A stranger who knew Rane far better than she.

She blocked out her first thought of him, face above hers in the firelight, the warm flame-glow tricking her into thinking the heat in his eyes meant they were one. A team.

Her anger rose up, hot as it had been this morning, at his leaving her. She pushed it aside, remembered how he'd looked the moment he'd run at the troll, blue blade gleaming.

"He is as true as his blade."

Under her hand, Soren relaxed a little.

"I have something here. A golden apple. I'm going to press it against you. It may heal you, if the spell Nuen cast in this chamber hasn't stripped it of its power."

"Spell?" As he asked the question, she pressed the apple against his skin.

As its cool, hard surface touched him, he gasped in reaction, and she remembered how she felt at the foot of the glass mountain, as the apple had healed the broken bones in her feet and legs.

She heard the faintest scuffle of sound behind her, such as men would make running in the dark, and suddenly blue light flooded the chamber, blinding her.

She cried out, pushing the apple even harder against Soren, her other arm coming up to shield her eyes.

Then she used her body to block Soren from anyone watching from the entrance to the massive room, felt for Soren's ragged pants, and slipped the apple into his pocket.

"Who are you?" His voice was quiet.

"Well spoken." A voice came from the entrance, and slowly, blessedly, the intensity of the light dimmed. "I am interested to know the answer to that question, too."

CHAPTER 24

The leaping blue flame shrunk to the size of a man's head and hovered in the center of the room. It cast an eerie glow over the chamber.

Nuen stood just within the entrance, long staff in hand. He was flanked by Jasper and the man Kayla had followed earlier.

Kayla saw Nuen was panting, his face slick with sweat. She wondered if it was from his run down the passage or the strain of manipulating the blue light.

A chain clinked beside her, and she turned her head, looked straight into Soren's eyes.

He was staring at her, but although he was still limp in his chains, a vitality radiated from him that hadn't been there before she'd touched him with the apple.

"Well, who are you?" Jasper spoke, harsh and impatient.

Kayla drew herself up. "I am surprised you don't recognize me, sir, as you were introduced to me just a few days ago by my father. And while you fawned over my hand, no doubt you were thinking of your scheme to steal the golden apple."

Jasper stepped back, mouth open.

There was a beat of silence. It seemed to go on and on.

"Who is she?" Nuen turned to Jasper, his lips tight with strain.

"Princess Kayla of Gaynor. It was her apple I sent Rane to win for me." Jasper reached out to steady himself against the cave wall.

Beside her, Soren moved, tensed, at the mention of Rane.

Nuen frowned. "What are you doing here?"

Nothing occurred to Kayla but the truth. What else was there? She said nothing.

"How are you not injured? I saw that bolt hit you. And how did you get in here undetected?" Nuen paused between each word, like an old man too tired to speak.

"The bolt missed, and I simply kept very quiet." She held her hands out, palms up.

"You have to be lying." Nuen lifted his staff.

"Wait!" Jasper grabbed his arm. "I have to think about this. This isn't some villager, Nuen, this is a political nightmare in the making."

"It doesn't need to be." Kayla opened her arms wider. "Rane De'Villier is above, with the golden apple. Bring his brother up, out into the open, and you can both get what you want."

Jasper's eyes darted to Nuen, then back to her. "Where is De'Villier?"

Kayla's lips twisted in contempt. "Where you won't find him. If you want the apple, Jasper, take Soren up where Rane can see him. What do you have to lose?"

"Why are you involved in this?" Jasper's eyes were narrow.

"You involved me in this." Kayla crossed her arms over her chest. Let some of the anger inside her show. "You know what winning the apple made Rane."

"What did it make him?" The question came from Soren, his gaze so focused on her, she blinked.

"It made him my betrothed." She dropped her arms to her sides and turned to face him. "It made me his."

It was Soren's turn to blink. His eyes widened.

Kayla spun back to the entrance, unable to meet his gaze.

"Unchain him." She held out her hand, as if she expected Jasper to place the key in it.

"No. She's not telling the truth. She must have used some magic to heal herself and make herself invisible. I saw that bolt hit her." Nuen took a step closer, and she watched a trickle of sweat slide down the unscarred side of his face. "And why would Rane let her come in here and rescue his brother. Surely he would have done it himself?"

"She's a princess, Nuen, not a witch. I've known of her, heard every piece of gossip about her, since I first started trading with Gaynor. She isn't magical." Jasper frowned, tapped his right fist into the open palm of his left hand. "But you have a point. Why would Rane leave the rescue to you?"

She lifted her shoulders. "Rane hasn't left anything to me. He's above, doing what he needs to do to make sure we can get out. Coming down here and releasing Soren is not the most dangerous part of his plan. It's the easiest. But when he sees me and his brother, he'll hand over the apple. He always planned to, after he rid himself of Eric the Bold's enchantment."

"Eric's involved in this?" Nuen glanced at Jasper, even more shaken than before.

Jasper shrugged. "He was there at the tournament, and Rane went off with him and then disappeared right after, with the apple in his possession. It's possible she's telling the truth."

"I am. And even if I'm not, what do you have to lose, in your own stronghold, surrounded by your men? With only me and Rane against you?" Kayla let her voice drip with derision.

Jasper stared at her, taking her measure, scoring up a grudge she knew he would never forget. "She's right. We have nothing to lose." He gave a nod to his silent lieutenant, and the man walked forward.

Kayla stood aside as he set a key in the lock that held the chains suspended from rings in the wall.

Soren gave a cry as he dropped, hard, to the cave floor. He lay, gasping and curled into a ball, hugging himself.

Kayla knelt beside him, and he flinched at her touch. She knew he was healed, even though it seemed the apple could not add back the weight he had lost, so this must be surprise, confusion, and some very good acting.

"Shh. Let's go." She looked up at Jasper's man. "Help me move him?"

Even though Soren was gaunt with hunger he was still a big man—so like Rane that an unexpected, embarrassing tear slid down her cheek to see him so damaged, even if his weakness was feigned. A few minutes ago, it hadn't been.

Her tear splashed onto the dirty skin of his shoulder where his sleeve had been torn away from his shirt.

He turned his head, and she was ensnared by blue eyes, blazing with questions.

She slipped a hand under his arm, making sure she was on the side she'd placed the golden apple. Jasper's lieutenant took his other arm.

As they lifted him to his feet, he took his own weight, hunched over like an old man, and again, Kayla had the sense he was stronger than he appeared. He leaned on her heavily, but there was a readiness to him, a tension in his frame, that made his weight easier to bear than if he'd been truly weak.

As her foot crossed the threshold from the cave to the passage, wild magic curled around her, like tendrils of fern, touching her with soft fronds, reaching out from the forest in silk-thin strands. It was invisible, or so fine, it could not be seen, but she shot a nervous look at her hands. There was the faintest purple sparkle at the tips, and she hid them in the folds of Soren's ripped shirt sleeves.

She needed more control over the magic, but she didn't know if Ylana would ever help her, now.

The way back up the spiraling tunnel seemed longer than the way down. She was gasping under Soren's weight by the time they stepped through the burnt ground floor of the tower and out into the night.

Jasper's man stepped away from Soren, hand going to his sword as if he expected Rane to leap out at them, and Soren pretended to stagger hard against her.

He shot her a look, and she gave a little shake of her head. She needed him to pretend weakness a little longer. She needed time to work out how to get them out.

142

She eased him to the ground, felt him tense. Ready to jump up.

She turned her gaze over the stockade fence to the forest beyond. She could feel wild magic, tight-woven balls of power, just within the trees. They'd been banished to the forest by the sorcerers who'd created them—caged there—but the spell-wall that hemmed them in was porous.

It was all around her. Although, perhaps not enough of it for what she would need to do.

She imagined tendrils of it drifting, fine as a spider's thread, through whatever gaps they could, gathering in her hands.

Someone lunged at her from behind, grabbing her right wrist and spinning her round. She cried out, tried to jerk her arm back.

It was Nuen, and from the corner of her eye, she saw Soren draw his feet under him, ready to spring.

Nuen yanked her forward, pushing up her sleeve. She curled her sparking fingers into a tight fist.

He held a torch, and as he lowered it to look, the heat of the flames was almost unbearable.

"Well?" Jasper asked him. "Satisfied?"

"She's no witch." Nuen peered closer. "But there is something there. I've never seen that pattern before."

Kayla jerked her arm out of his grasp, took a deep step back. She jammed her hands into her pockets.

The time had come to escape. And she didn't care if she had to burn the whole stronghold to the ground to do it.

CHAPTER 25

"*W*here is Rane?" Jasper made a movement with his hand, and Kayla heard the sound of crossbows being cocked. She looked over her shoulder, saw a line of men on the guard's walk, bows pointed straight at her.

"It isn't Rane you have to worry about." As she spoke, she thought herself invisible, felt the surge of power within her, and dived across to Soren, her hand clamping his arm, making him invisible, too.

But as he faded, something struck them both, a flash of blue, and Kayla saw she was visible again, her spell stripped away.

Nuen gripped his staff, white-knuckled, his face contorted with effort.

"Stop her." Jasper's call to his crossbowmen was tinged with panic.

As the first arrows flew, Kayla turned, lifted her hands. Purple light flared. She felt a tug as wild magic poured through her, felt the exhilaration as the arrows fell useless, clattering on the cobbles.

There was a moment of silence. She turned back to Nuen, excitement, power, thrumming in her chest.

Nuen stared at her, mouth open.

She raised her hands, felt the wild magic flying from the forest to her, thin and sharp as wire, until she had a ball of it hovering over each hand.

She glanced at the archers and ripped their bows from their hands, flung them up and over the wall into the forest. Smashed them into the ground.

She was shaking with reaction, with the force of wild magic power.

"Kill her." Jasper took a step closer to Nuen.

A look passed between them, and Kayla knew Nuen didn't have the power. He was drained.

Soren rose up beside her, and she took a step toward the gate, her eyes never leaving the brothers.

"Let's go." Her hands sparked again, and the gates blew open, the heavy wooden bar holding them together exploding into splinters.

Soren faced the gate, then stopped, frozen, beside her.

"What is it?" She risked a glance over her shoulder, and saw Sooty streak through the open entrance, hackles raised, her eyes gleaming gold in the torch-light.

As Kayla turned back, Nuen lifted his staff, but before she could cry out, before she could do anything, he struck. Not at her, at Soren.

The flash of blue knocked him off his feet, throwing him through the air to land hard on his back. Kayla ran to him, and Sooty leapt past her, snarling, at Jasper and Nuen.

"Had my hand on the apple." Soren was already struggling to his feet. "But—"

"No time." Kayla gripped Soren's arm, saw Sooty had cornered the brothers against the tower wall. She called to the cat, and Sooty turned immediately, ran in a loping stride toward her.

"Wait. The golden apple . . ." Soren lunged at something on the ground, but Nuen was already drawing back his arm, staff in hand, and as Sooty slammed against her side, she wished them, in a fireworks of purple, to the safety of the forest.

THEY LANDED hard and fast in the abandoned clearing. Soren was in mid-lunge, and he hit the ground, rolled and came up, snarling.

Sooty snarled back, took a step toward him.

Soren stopped short, his whole posture still with shock. "Where are we?" He looked around. "What is that?" He pointed to Sooty, and she spat at him.

"I sent us into the forest, and this is Sooty." Kayla rubbed Sooty's head, humming to her. Her hands shook and she was breathless, her hums coming in short, sharp bursts. She felt as if an ogre had shaken her, and she was still vibrating from it.

"How did Nuen miss that you're a witch?"

Kayla tried to lift her shoulders in a shrug and winced at their stiffness. "I'm not a witch he's ever seen before. I don't use earth magic."

"You use that?" Soren's voice was hard, now, and she saw he was pointing between the trees. A sphere of wild magic moved into view.

She nodded. "I use that." She knelt beside Sooty, and scratched under her chin.

"You have to send me back to Jasper." Soren watched the wild magic, his stance shifting as it moved, always keeping it in front of him.

"Why do you want me to do that?" Kayla sat back on her heels, her mouth open.

"Because I dropped the golden apple when Nuen hit me with that blast of blue." Soren curled his hands into fists at his sides. "I tried to tell you—"

"Nuen was about to strike, his arm was already back. If I hadn't taken us away, he'd have hit you."

"Well, send me back now. I'll get it." He spun with the wild magic as it circled the clearing.

"If Nuen has found the golden apple, neither of us can go back there. I only managed to get us out because he was weak. I think we can be sure that is no longer the case." She rose, clenching her own fists. "It is very, very unfortunate that Jasper has the golden apple now. Very unfortunate."

"You think I don't know that?" At last, Soren turned his back on the wild magic and faced her. "I'll go back anyway. Steal it."

Kayla took a deep breath, gritted her teeth. "You'd undo everything I've just done, getting you out?"

He shrugged. "What choice do I have?"

Kayla crossed her hands under her breasts and beside her, Sooty flicked her tail in anger. "Jasper is not our biggest problem. That honor goes to Eric the Bold, and Rane has gone off to face him alone."

Soren stilled at the mention of his brother's name. "Why would Rane go off to confront Eric the Bold?"

"He didn't have a choice. To get the golden apple," she glared at Soren, "to free *you*, he placed himself under Eric's power. Now that he'd accomplished what Eric wanted, he's gone back to have the enchantment lifted."

"What did he have to do?" Soren's eyes were narrow.

"He had to steal a magical gem."

"And how do you know so much about this? Why are you here?"

Stung by his tone, after everything she'd done for him, she drew herself up. "I know so much because I got caught up in Rane's enchantment. I'm in this as deep as he is."

"Does Rane know you can control wild magic?" He spoke slowly.

"He does."

"I can't see him being happy about it. Can't see him being mixed up with you at all to tell the truth, *princess*."

Kayla stared at him. She saw her hands were sparking, and she held them out in front of her. Tilted them this way and that, watching the play of light. "You De'Villier boys are very hard-pressed to express gratitude, aren't you?"

He moved, uncomfortable for the first time. "What did you do for Rane?"

"Besides ensnaring myself in Eric's enchantment to help him save you?" She thought of what she'd given to Rane, and clamped tight on her jaw. "Never mind."

The wild magic sphere drifted closer, leaving the trees to move into the clearing, and its purple light threw deep shadows under Soren's cheekbones, across his collarbone, stark and prominent. Her anger and frustration were suddenly gone.

Jasper had been starving him to death.

She caught sight of the abandoned bags, and crouched beside them, belatedly remembering she'd left her own, with all the food, just outside Jasper's fortress.

She thought of the spot, and suddenly she was there, her bags just in front of her. She gasped, finding it hard to breathe. Jasper's fortress loomed up—a silent, solid wall of darkness. She laid a hand on the bags, listened for a moment. Nothing.

She wished herself back in the clearing, and as she appeared, still in a crouch, Sooty knocked her over.

"Hey!" She lay on her back, and Soren stood over her, fury in his eyes.

"Where did you go?"

"I remembered I left my bags with all the food just outside Jasper's. I didn't realize I'd be able to go there and back so easily." She sat up, looked across at the wild magic sphere. "Must be all the wild magic around."

Sooty rubbed against her shoulder, and she smiled. "Miss me, did you?" She glanced at Soren. "I was gone for all of one minute."

Soren held out a hand, and she took it, allowed him to pull her to her feet.

"It felt longer than that. I didn't know what had happened to you." He dropped her hand like it was hot the moment she was standing.

She still held the bags, and she dipped into one, rifled through them for something she thought he could hold down after so long without food and held out a hunk of bread. She saw the wariness in his eyes. And the hunger.

"Your brother trusts me. He left the golden apple with me, his only means of getting you back." She did not look away from him, and at last, he gave a nod and tugged the bread from her hand. Bit into it.

He crouched beside the bags left in the clearing, and pulled out a few changes of clothes. Kayla watched him rub a cloak thought-fully between finger and thumb.

"What happened to these men?"

"I don't know." Kayla shrugged. "The bags were here earlier."

He turned the packs over, looked at them more closely, and Kayla had a sense he'd seen them before. Knew their owners. "Where do we find Eric?"

"I last saw him in Gaynor. That's the only place I can think of to start." Sooty butted Kayla's legs, and she shook herself. "I think Gaynor is that way. I suppose I can use wild magic to get us to the edge of the forest where Rane and I started. The horses might even still be there." She pointed to a path on the other side of the clearing.

Soren looked down at the packs again. "What would have the power to make five or more men vanish into thin air? And what were they doing back here, so close to the stronghold? At least two guards taunted me with the fact they were going out to hunt for Rane."

A cold, sick feeling settled over Kayla, and she dropped suddenly to her knees, pawing through all the packs, looking for a sign that Rane had been here.

He couldn't have been caught in the gem's power, he couldn't . . .

Soren laid a hand on her shoulder, and crouched beside her. "What is it?"

Only the fear on his face brought her back to herself, because she saw it was fear of her.

"The gem. If it's touched, it sends out a blast of power. I was able to shield myself from it when I took it from Ylana, but if these men managed to capture Rane, and they searched him . . ."

"They would have searched him." Soren spoke with grim certainty. "But Rane's things aren't here. I already looked, to see if you were lying to me."

She nodded, uncaring of his distrust. She only cared that Rane was safe. "The gem isn't here, either, and it would be, if everyone was caught in its blast. Someone's taken it, someone who knows not to touch it." She remembered Sooty sniffing on the other side of the large log on one side of the fireplace and walked over to it. Turned back to look at the cut ropes near the packs.

"Rane saw what they were going to do, and shielded himself behind the log. Then he got his knife out of the packs and cut his ropes and carried on. The enchantment would compel him to."

Soren joined her, looking at the ground beside the log, and then walked back to the ropes. "This was Rane's knife, no question. Nothing cuts like that thing."

He looked around at the empty clearing again. "Does Eric know what this gem does? Did he warn you what would happen when you touched it?"

She shook her head. "He didn't and it would have served no purpose for him to send us to our deaths. I don't doubt for a moment he truly wants it. He must have heard it is powerful, but he doesn't know the nature of that power."

"What will happen if he touches it?"

Kayla reached out and rubbed Sooty's head. "I don't know. Perhaps he can protect himself like I did. Perhaps he can direct it, or use it some other way. He's powerful, more powerful than I am." She gave a dry laugh. "I barely know what I'm doing."

"And Rane is giving this thing to him?" There was plain disbelief in Soren's voice.

"What choice does he have?" Her voice was hot with indignation. "As far as he knows, if he doesn't he can't rescue you. Which is why we need to find him as quickly as we can. Let him know you're safe."

Soren stood, stiff and angry, and then gave a reluctant nod.

"Can you tell which way Rane went?" She lifted a hand and wished for a light, and felt the minute pull of wild magic as a bright ball of light hovered over her palm.

Soren glared at her, as if using wild magic was a direct insult to him, but he walked slowly around the clearing with her following behind, light held high, and eventually pointed down a narrow path. "Here."

"Then we follow."

He nodded, and they both turned back to the clearing to collect their things.

Soren pulled his ripped shirt over his head, put on a clean one. She had to turn her eyes away from the way his ribs pressed against his skin.

"Lead the way." He stood slowly, shoving extra clothes into a bag and slinging it over his shoulder. He moved like an old man to join them on the path. It must be hunger and fatigue, because the apple had healed him of all his injuries.

Sooty went first. The spheres of wild magic moved with them, sinuously twisting through the trees.

Kayla was glad she had them as her allies.

"Rane and I used to chase wild magic, in the beginning. But even actively looking for them, we only ever saw one at a time." There was a sudden anger in his voice, and as she turned, he grabbed her shoulder, forcing her to stop. He gestured away from the path. "Just how many do you see?" He gave her a little shake. "How many?"

The strength and frustration in his hands made her afraid, and before she could think it through, her fingers glowed.

Soren was suddenly five strides away, suspended in the air, his face white with shock.

She looked, right to left, and saw perhaps twenty or more spheres on either side of her. An endless supply of power.

"Don't surprise me like that again." She was shaking; exhaustion, nerves, adrenalin rolling through her in waves. She released him, and he dropped hard onto the ground.

She watched him get warily to his feet.

"Just what are you? What have you done to my brother?" Soren rubbed a hand over his face. "What is going on?"

Kayla stared at him, the sparks on her fingertips fading away. She turned back to the path. "When I find out, I'll let you know."

CHAPTER 26

*R*ane had run through the night.

He'd stopped once, to drink and eat, and snatch two hours of sleep, then the enchantment forced him on. Now, as he reached the light-filled edges of the forest, he felt strangely removed from his body, as if exhaustion and hunger had pushed out his soul to make more room for themselves.

He must be close. His burden was getting lighter and lighter every hour, as if he carried a sack full of seed on his shoulders, and with every step, more leaked out of a hole in the corner.

But as he stepped away from the trees and looked down into a valley on the border of Gaynor and its northern neighbor, Klevan, he could see nothing.

No grand castle, no tower, no sign of Eric at all.

A wide strip of open field, lush and thick with summer grass, ran on either side of a river curling through the valley. Low bush and trees clung higher up the valley's sides, until they blended with the solid wall of forest at the top.

He walked down, weaving his way through the rocks and bushes, toward the river. It was approaching midday, and the air was hot, the sun strong now he no longer had the protective canopy of the trees to shield him.

The river glinted, diamond-studded, in the sunlight, and Rane picked up his pace, eager for the feel of cold water on his skin.

He'd kept silent as he'd walked down from the forest, out of habit and out of caution, and he slipped into the water quietly, too, leaving his pack and boots tucked against a rock.

He submerged his body, sank down until the water covered his head. He was weightless, cool. The water tugged at his clothes, soaking the stains and dirt of days in the forest off him.

The current had pulled him downstream, spun him round, and he rose up, slowly, reluctantly, anchoring his feet on the stony riverbed. He surfaced, facing the way he'd come, and as he blinked the water from his eyes, he saw someone . . . something . . . leaning over his pack.

He froze, letting the water pull him into the shadow of the river bank, sinking down as low as he could. He wished for his moon-stone, feeling its loss like a knife cut.

Whatever creature was rifling through his things, it had thin limbs, a barrel body and knobbly head, and stood perhaps head and shoulders taller than himself. Its skin was a turnip-like shade of purple.

It muttered something over and over in a soft voice, then turned its head, sharply, down river.

Rane held his breath. It seemed to be looking straight at him. Another moment ticked by, and then it turned back to the pack, lifted out a piece of dried meat and gnawed on it, loudly and appreciatively.

Rane pulled out his knife. Began to move against the current, staying close to the river bank. There was an overhang of bushes between himself and the creature, and when he reached it, he pulled himself up behind the cover of foliage, water streaming off him.

He edged around the bush, knife raised.

The creature had gone.

He straightened from his crouch, cautious and wary, his eyes going to the river.

Something grabbed him from behind, and he let out a shout that echoed up the valley. He flung his arm back and up, knife blade gleaming bright blue.

"Shh. Shh. Ow!"

His brain registered the shushing and his hand tried to pull back from the stab.

The creature let go of him, releasing his hold as if he were a scorpion and Rane rolled, coming up with blade ready.

The creature stepped back, nursing its arm and watching him with accusing eyes.

"Sorry." He slammed the blade back in its sheath. "I'm sorry. I thought you were attacking me." He took a step closer and the thing drew back, holding its arm as far from him as it could.

"I'm really sorry. I have bandages in my pack, let me help you." He didn't wait for an answer, he leaned over and grabbed his bag, unfastening a strap and pulling out neat white bandages and ointment. Gaynor Castle's doctor had packed them, in case Kayla was scratched or hurt. He'd left most of them with her, but had taken a few for himself.

He held out his hand, and the creature watched him, its huge eyes unblinking. The irises were a pale yellow, almost gold, startling against the purple skin.

"Come. Please." He held up the bandages. "I'll bind it."

The creature gave a sniff, then gingerly extended its arm. The cut was deep, and Rane reached out his hand, took the arm gently.

The creature flinched at his touch.

"It's all right. I won't hurt you." He applied the salve to skin that was soft and crinkled under his fingertips. He wrapped the bandage tight.

He was so close to the creature, he smelled the dried meat it had taken from his pack on its breath, and the wet stone smell of the river. "What is your name?"

It twisted its arm this way and that, admiring the bandage. Then it smiled, and Rane had to force himself not to jerk back. Its teeth were sharp, the canines long, like a wolf's. "Shh." It lifted a long finger to its lips, then pointed down the valley. "Nasty, there."

"A nasty man? A nasty place?" Rane raised a hand to block the glare of midday sun, but he could see nothing.

"Hidden." It nodded. "Nasty man, nasty place."

"I have to go there." Rane pulled his boots toward him and tugged them on. His clothes had already started to dry in the heat, but in places they clung to him, damp and cool. He shivered as a light breeze blew down the valley.

"No, no, no, no, no." It clicked its tongue. "Nasty."

"I know it's nasty. Believe me, I know." Rane picked up his pack, delving around for another stick of dried meat. He held it out. "I still have to go. Will you show me?"

The thing shook its head, lifted a leg and pointed to a deep scar running from thigh to knee. "Nasty." It bared its teeth.

"I understand." Rane kept holding out the meat, and eventually, tentatively, it took the gift. "Sorry I cut you." He took out a spare bandage and the ointment, held them out as well.

The thing took them with delight, chortling and cradling them to its body.

Its face fell as Rane began walking in the direction it had pointed. "No. No."

Rane turned. "I have to."

It took a step toward him, then halted. "Bye, bye." It waved, its voice forlorn.

Rane returned the wave, then headed toward the open space where Eric's castle must be.

When he looked over his shoulder, it was still there, its hand raised in a salute. Whatever it was, it knew this place, knew Eric, even better than he did. And it did not think he would be coming back.

CHAPTER 27

here was something at the far end of the valley. Rane moved his head one way, then the other, trying to pin it down. Elusive as a shadow, it seems to always be on the move.

He came at it at an angle, circled it, rather than approaching it straight on, and it disappeared completely. Then, as he tightened the circle, slanted in, he felt the first cool touches of a mist on his face, and suddenly he was in a white fog, moisture beading his clothes and his face, clinging to his hair.

The quiet meadow sounds faded, the rush of the river, the rustle of grass. Silence took hold, squeezing everything else out, rendering him deaf and blind.

He stumbled, disoriented, and caught movement—fast, dark, furtive. Something ran across his path.

He crouched, lowering his bags quietly to the ground, his knife already out, his thumb just over the dragon.

He moved sideways, still low to the ground, deeper into the mist. Something came at him again, the fog swirling and eddying around it as it ran straight for where he had been.

He heard a grunt of anger, then a growl, and every hair on the back of his neck lifted.

Whatever hunted him, it was not human.

He was so close to it, he could smell it, the cold, black smell of dark lakes far below ground.

Eric had dug deep to find this guard dog.

It went very still, the moment stretching out. He could feel it listening, and then it sniffed the air.

Rane tensed, waiting for it to come to him. Felt the moment it turned his way, nostrils flared. He rose from his crouch, knees still bent, ready.

It sprang, silent, and as it leaped, Rane brought his thumb down on the dragon. The blade lengthened to sword-length and the creature screamed, howled, as the tip slid into its flesh. It thrashed against the pain, and Rane's arms were wrenched as it fought the knife.

He hauled back, pulling the knife out and up. He swung it across where he thought the throat was, and with a gurgle, the beast fell.

Rane stepped closer, crouched beside it, and the fog cleared a little. It was a grindylow. It lay dead, its shaggy green hair matted, its mouth drawn back in a rigid snarl.

He'd only seen one once, when he was twelve, by a stream. The grindylow had risen from the dark, weed-clogged water, hands tipped with sharp nails, clawing for him. He'd leapt back, run from it, and it had not pursued him.

But this was no woodland stream grindylow. This one had a dark, almost black-green pelt, and it was huge.

But more surprising, it was far from any stream. The river was behind Rane. The grindylow had approached from the front. What water source had it come from?

From the smell of it, someplace stagnant and deep.

Rane rose, knife held out, thumb just off the dragon. Every step he took was careful.

Something loomed in the mist, and he went down on his haunches, edging forward slowly.

It was a well.

A sound, the slither and scrape of claws on stone, came from the right. He stayed very still, eyes straining in the swirling white. For just one moment, the fog parted and he saw a second grindylow crouched beside another well. Its focus was ahead, and it moved off, quiet and lethal.

There was a change in the light in front of him, and Rane caught a brief glimpse of blue sky between the two wells.

They were the pillars of a gateway.

His heart beat faster as the realization came to him.

Eric was almost in his reach.

SOOTY WAITED FOR THEM, tail flicking impatiently. She'd run after a hare, its scream short and sharp, and now it lay discarded, a bloody mess beside her on the path. She was panting in the heat.

Kayla watched her with heavy, burning eyes, and tried to infuse her own step with a little of the bounding joy of her cat.

Soren trudged behind her, silent and withdrawn. He still didn't trust her and he hated the wild magic that followed them.

He'd taken to counting it, muttering the number under his breath, as if each new sphere was another mark against her, but he'd tired of the game. Or there were no new spheres to count. Perhaps they had all the spheres in the forest with them.

Kayla looked around and thought it might be possible. There were certainly a hundred or more. An army of them.

She knew he thought he was dealing with the enemy. That he was consorting with the one thing he and Rane had fought against, betraying both himself and his brother.

She reached Sooty, found herself unable to resist sitting down. She leaned against a tree and watched Soren as he walked toward her.

He said nothing, but sank down against a tree of his own.

"We both need sleep. We can't go on without rest." She'd known it. Soren had known it. And still, they had not stopped to rest since they left the clearing, walking through the night, and as the dawn broke, and as the morning sun began to heat the air.

They had followed the trail Rane had made, the way easy to see because he'd had to fight his way along the overgrown path, and there were signs of his passage everywhere.

Kayla wondered where he was going. To Eric's castle? Eric would not have waited in Gaynor for their return. He would want to be on his own territory, behind his own walls. He'd want no one to know about or understand his advantage, would want privacy when they brought him the gem.

It seemed to her, though, that they must be much slower than Rane, compelled by the enchantment and fit as he was. And she was desperate to get to him before he approached Eric.

Time was running out.

She slid down to the soft forest floor, curled up, and heard Sooty shuffle until she was pressed up against Kayla's back.

Kayla opened an eye, saw Soren leaning against his tree, eyes closed.

They were right on the path, dangerously exposed, but they had Sooty to watch them, and they could go no further.

She lay, half-awake, half dreaming, and sunk slowly into the blissful black of sleep.

She would have sworn she was only under for a few minutes at most, but when the shout woke her, the first thing she noticed was the long afternoon shadows. Her mouth was dry, and a headache pounded her skull.

Sooty had not left her side, and she sat, alert, ears pointed forward.

The shout came again, and with a start, Kayla realized it was Soren.

As she stood, he started screaming.

She ran toward the sound, Sooty beside her. Something moved, quick and sly, to the side of her, and heart pounding, Kayla turned her head to look.

It was a sphere of wild magic.

Her fear eased, and she ignored it, concentrating on running without tripping as she kept pace with Sooty along the narrow track. It was off the main path, and Kayla wondered why Soren had come down here.

His screams cut off abruptly and she was at last able to hear the hiss of a river. Her throat convulsed at the thought of cool, fresh water, and she understood why he had taken this path.

She burst out of the trees onto the bank of a wide stream, and stopped just short of a mud-slicked battleground. The smell of fresh clay and water hung in the air.

A tall, lithe woman was sitting straddled over Soren's chest. Her body was covered in scratches and mud, her thin white dress torn, exposing a perfect breast.

Soren hadn't been easily subdued.

One of their packs was lying beside the river, and Soren's face was smooth shaven again, his shirt off as if he'd been washing when the woman had attacked him.

As Kayla watched, the woman pressed a long, sharpened stick into the joint between his arm and shoulder. A thin, weak sound came from his throat and Soren pushed at her with ineffectual hands.

The woman pulled back and Kayla noticed webbing between her fingers. Her feet had splayed, webbed toes.

"Stop!"

The woman jerked, turned an astonishingly beautiful face to Kayla.

Beside Kayla, Sooty hissed, arching her back.

The woman rose to her feet, quick and graceful as a bird, her eyes on Sooty. She stepped over Soren, closer to the water. Soren rolled away from her, toward Kayla.

"He is yours?" The woman's voice was not a voice, but the sound of water gurgling and bubbling, strung together to make words.

Kayla shook her head. "He's the brother of the one who is mine."

"Then give him back to me."

Kayla shook his head again. "You were hurting him."

The woman laughed, a twisted, babbling brook of a laugh. "Yes. I was hurting him." She lunged, suddenly, at Soren, her long, slender arms reaching for him, and Kayla's hands flashed.

The woman leapt back, crying out, her right hand cradled in her left.

Kayla was unsure what she had done. Burnt her? Stung her? She did not even know how she had managed to react so quickly.

Something touched Kayla from behind, and she risked a quick look. Saw the wild magic sphere that had followed her was right behind her, nudging her. It rose up, just behind and a little above her head.

When she turned back, the woman was gone.

"Can you walk?" Kayla crouched beside Soren. He'd dragged himself to her, and she wondered what was wrong with his legs.

"Can't feel my legs." He was gasping for air, as if his ribs were broken, and his lips didn't move as he spoke. "Can't feel anywhere she touched. It's all cold." His body shook.

Kayla cursed for the hundredth time that they did not have the apple. She put a hand on his leg. Pictured the cold seeping out of it. Her hand glowed.

Soren raised his gaze to hers. "That worked."

She did the other leg, his chest, his arms. "Where else?"

He touched his face, and she placed a hand flat against each cheek. She could not look at him, it seemed . . . too intimate, so she closed her eyes as she wished him warm again.

He drew his first deep, normal, breath, and she opened her eyes again. Was caught in a gaze so like Rane's her heart thundered.

"Thank you." He pushed away from her, and stood.

She stood with him and they both looked toward the stream.

"She's still there. I can feel her." Soren's fists clenched.

"What is she?"

He looked at her strangely. "She's an asrai. A water spirit."

Kayla blinked. He spoke as if it were common knowledge. Well, not in the royal household of Gaynor. "I've never heard of them."

"If I walk toward the edge, she'll leap out to get me. When she does, will you do something to her? So she cannot get anyone else?"

Kayla did not look at him, keeping her eyes on the water. "You like giving yourself up for sacrifice, don't you? Burning Nuen's tower, wanting to go back for the apple. Now this."

He shrugged. "Will you?"

She didn't know if she could, but her fingers tingled, and she felt the charge in the air above her head from the wild magic. "Yes."

Sooty's gaze had not wavered from the asrai since they'd first seen her, and Kayla looked down, saw she was looking to the left. "She's over there." She pointed.

Without another word, without a single hesitation or break in his stride, Soren walked to the part of the bank she'd indicated.

The asrai sprang, water streaming off her white blonde hair, pressing the translucent fabric of her dress to her body. Her mouth was drawn back in a snarl, and she screamed as she leapt forward.

Kayla felt a surge of power. Shock at the explosiveness of the asrai's attack, fear for Soren, fizzed through her, and the force of wild magic she drew threw her hands out in front of her. A flash of purple blinded her and the asrai's scream turned into the cry of a bird. When she blinked away the spots in front of her eyes, Soren was jumping back as a heron stabbed at him with its long, sharp beak.

Sooty crouched down, growling low, and the heron stopped its attack. It leapt clumsily, wings flapping, into the air.

Soren said nothing as he watched it fly over the trees and disappear. He stood, cool and calm as ever. "Are you ready to continue on?"

Kayla let her gaze drift from the point where the bird disappeared, and drew in a deep breath. She had just turned an asrai into a bird. She'd thought when she'd seen it stabbing a stick at Soren how like a heron it had looked. Somehow, the wild magic had taken that thought, made it real. Or was it her? Her doing entirely?

She took another deep breath. "I'm ready, but I think we are wasting too much time. Time we don't have. I said the last time I saw Eric, he was in Gaynor, but I've just remembered, that isn't true . . ." Kayla let her words trail off. Turned to the sphere behind her. It was directly at eye level.

"I think . . ." Her voice trembled. "I think I have just remembered a short cut."

CHAPTER 28

*H*e burst through the mist, and suddenly he could see the massive keep that dominated the landscape, standing on the slope at the far end of the valley.

Behind him, the fog had gone, and so had the wells. So had his bags. Like his approach on the other side of it, if he moved his head he caught the opening from the corner of his eye.

From thin air, he heard a keening sound and shivered. The second grindylow had just found its fallen companion.

Time to go.

As he approached the massive wooden double-door of the keep, he wondered how Eric thought to get the gem. Had he instructed the grindylows to kill everyone who came through the mist, and bring him the bodies to search?

Eric had never intended to lift the enchantment. Never intended to let them live. Or never intended to let *him* live. He had no idea how the grindylows would have dealt with Kayla.

He thought Eric's interest in Kayla too intense for him to want her dead. Then he remembered the strange encounter Kayla had with Eric in the forest. Rane did not know what had been said between them. Perhaps Eric had decided Kayla would never be compliant enough.

He reached the stairs, climbed them to the double doors and lifted his hand. Before he grasped the knocker, shaped like a lightning bolt, he paused. Tried to strip his soul of any softness. Any pity.

The only way to come out of this free of enchantment—to come out of this alive—was to be as hard as the gem strapped to the small of his back.

"IT IS HERE, SOMEWHERE." Kayla looked at the sea of spheres hovering in front of her. She had called them to her, like she called Sooty, and they had come.

That they *had* come, that she had that power, was too big for her to think about. Instead, she concentrated on finding the sphere that had given her access to Eric's dungeon.

"What do you mean, it's here?" Soren leaned against a tree, arms crossed over his chest, and Kayla felt a slow, deep-burning anger at him. How many times must she save him before he trusted her?

"I mean," she spoke each word carefully, as flat as she could, "that one of these wild magic spheres was created when Eric cast a spell in his dungeon. Somehow, it is still connected to its place of creation. It gave me a window to step through before, right into Eric's castle."

Soren stood straight, forehead creased. "You think you can call forward the right one?"

Kayla lifted a hand. "I don't know. But even if I have to touch every single one, it will be quicker than wasting time we don't have following Rane's trail."

She closed her eyes. Thought back to the night she'd found herself in Eric's lair. She'd run down the path, away from the woman in the clearing, and wild magic had blocked her path, stretched into a flat oval.

Had it been offering her an escape?

She shook her head, opened her eyes. One sphere moved, darting between the others toward her.

She held her breath, and as it stopped in front of her, it flattened, stretched, into a window. She leaned forward, and saw the stairs, heard the faint drip of water off the walls.

"Kayla?"

She breathed out at last. Turned to him. "Run back to the main path and get my bag. We have a way in."

Soren looked at the glimmering oval. "You want me to go through there?" His mouth set in a hard line.

She was at the end of her patience. "Do what you like. It obviously means nothing to you that your brother is through there because he's trying to save your life. Leave him to his fate, stay here and count spheres of wild magic. Throw yourself at every dangerous creature you can find. Offer yourself up to Jasper for more torture. Whatever makes you happy."

His head snapped in her direction, his mouth open.

She turned and stalked away, back to the main path.

"Wait!" There was a note of panic in his voice. "Where are you going?"

She looked over her shoulder. "To get my bag."

He shook his head. Pushed past her, his body stiff with frustration.

"Stay here. I'll get the cursed bag."

CHAPTER 29

$\mathcal{R}$ ane let the knocker fall. After his deliberate silence, its crack made him wince.

There was no response.

He slammed it against the door again.

Footsteps sounded, quick and strong.

The door swung back and Eric stood before him. His face was emotionless, but Rane noticed a tick in the corner of his left eye, and felt a surge of satisfaction.

"Where is the princess?" Eric looked beyond him.

Rane felt something dark and ugly crawl over his skin at the eager look in Eric's eyes. "Why would I bring her to you?"

Eric shoved him aside, stepped outside and looked around. "Where is she? She must be here. The enchantment won't allow for anything else."

"She isn't here. And if she had come with me, what would those grindylows have done to her? What they tried to do to me?"

Eric turned slowly, his eyes moving over the fields, as if unable to let go of the certainty Kayla was here. "No. Their instructions have always been to kill only men. All women are to be brought to me."

"I never realized grindylows were so easily commanded."

Eric sneered. "They are not normal grindylows. They are creatures of my . . . tinkering."

Rane fought down his distaste. He thought he heard another howl of grief from the empty field.

"She must be dead." Eric spoke slowly, then cocked his head to one side, as if he heard the howl, too. "That is the only way it makes sense. Kayla is dead."

Rane raised his hands as if in surrender. "Yes."

Eric gave a cry of rage, and leapt, staff swinging back. Not for a spell. He wanted to strike a physical blow.

Rane leapt out of Eric's way, ducking into the hallway of the castle, hand reaching for his knife.

Before he could, he was grabbed from behind, his arms pinned to his sides, and as he struggled to get free, Eric lunged again, his staff connecting with Rane's shoulder.

Rane roared with pain. He twisted and bucked against the arms holding him, hitting the massive body behind with elbows and head. The hold tightened, crushing his chest, and Rane saw the green-grey arms of a stone giant. He stilled in shock, letting his body go limp.

"You thought I was alone?" Eric slammed his staff into Rane's abdomen, and Rane gritted his teeth to stop calling out.

He had hoped Eric would be alone, but he'd never counted on it. A stone giant, though . . . Despair clawed at him, weighed him down. They were fast, incredibly strong. Almost impossible to beat. He could smell the hot energy of it, the stink of iron, enveloping him as he stood trapped in its arms.

"Where's the gem?" Eric brought his face right up to Rane's, his dark eyes blazing on the edge of control.

Rane took as deep a breath as he could with the tight hold the stone giant had on his chest. Braced himself in advance for the retaliation. "Let me go, first."

Eric struck, hitting him in the midriff again with his staff. "You have no power to bargain. Where is it?"

Rane closed his eyes, as if in defeat. "In my bags. I left them in the mists with the grindylows."

Eric stepped back. "Find them," he said to the stone giant. He lifted his staff, and as Rane was released, blue light flashed.

He was paralyzed again, just as he had been on the jousting field of Gaynor Castle. The stone giant stepped around him and down the stairs. It was double his size, stocky, every inch rippling with muscle. It wore nothing but a leather flap from its waist, and Rane saw its back was scarred with burns.

"Come with me." Eric stepped into the hallway, and Rane's body followed him, jerkily, like a badly-played marionette.

To be so out of control . . . Rane tried to clear a calm space in his mind, to get over the rage that was a conflagration within. He needed a cool head. To conserve his energy, not fight a battle he couldn't win.

"This drives you mad, doesn't it?" Eric waited for him, his face twisted in a mixture of rage and gloating. "Every step I make you take barely shaves the edge off my fury. I know you must have had her, and the thought of your filthy woodsman's hands on her . . ." Eric clenched his fists, swallowed convulsively. "She was *mine*. I saw what she was and I forced an agreement from her father. And then you . . ." He lifted his staff, and Rane had time only to understand Eric had finally lost control.

Blue light hit him, sent him flying through the air. He slammed into the wall at the far end of the hallway, and lay, crumpled, paralyzed, the world shrinking around him, with darkness framing his vision.

He heard Eric walking to him, the footsteps faint, as if coming from far away. He could not move, could only watch Eric's black boots come closer and closer. Watch, helpless, as his foot drew back and slammed into his face.

CHAPTER 30

S ooty would not go through the wild magic sphere, and Kayla stepped through without her. The cold of the stone stairwell enveloped her, a shock after the steamy heat of the forest.

Sooty leaned forward, as if looking into a fishpond, and tapped at the sphere with her massive paw. It dipped through the shimmering light into the stairwell, and with a chirp, Sooty pulled it back. Her whole body shivered.

Kayla crouched low, looking up the stairs to make sure no-one was coming, and then crept round the curve on the wall and peered around it to see what was beyond.

Last time, it had been unlit, but it wasn't dark anymore.

Light flickered from torches along both walls, and Kayla realized how massive the chamber was.

Something hung, strung up by its arms, head bowed, much as Soren had been, to her left, quite close, and she leaned forward, trying to get a better look.

It was dark purple, tall, and painfully thin. Its back was to her, and she could see burn marks across its shoulders.

There was a clink of metal, and with a start, Kayla noticed Eric, standing with a gray-green giant, at the far end of the room.

They were wrapping chains around something—someone—and Kayla risked rising up a little, straining to see who it was . . .

Rane.

Her heart seized in her chest, the pain forcing her to press a fist into her ribs.

She began forward then stopped short. Where was Soren? He'd been right behind her. A mix of panic and anger rose up in her, choked her, as she realized he hadn't come through.

She edged back to the stairwell to see if she would really have to do this alone.

As she rounded the corner, Sooty jumped through, crouching as low as Kayla on the icy stone floor.

Wherever they were, it stood to reason they were not in the Great Forest. Eric had seemed genuinely afraid of it, back at Gaynor Castle. So it followed there would be no wild magic to draw on here.

She peered out of the oval, to the forest beyond, and tried to draw power to her through the portal. It came reluctantly, she could feel the resistance as it passed through the shimmering purple light. Her hands sparked, but she was getting a sense now of how much power she had available at any one time, and she knew she couldn't do much with what was coming through to her.

There was a groan from the room beyond, a half-conscious sound, and she crept back to look, still pulling all the power she could.

Eric had stepped back from the table, and the massive giant was pulling on a chain she hadn't noticed, levering Rane up. His eyes were closed and his face swollen, his eyes puffy and black. He hung from the ceiling like a rag doll.

Rage, pure and elemental, ran through her in a scorching wild-fire, and she heard the air crackle as wild magic flickered and writhed from the forest through the sphere to her.

It formed a small ball just above her shoulder, spinning fast as her anger.

More. She needed as much as she could get.

She glanced back at the sphere, and saw with a little dip in her stomach that it was shrinking. Her window was using itself up. And pulling wild magic through it seemed to drain its energy even faster.

She looked for a way to get closer that would shield her from Eric's view, and as she braced herself, ready to go, someone dropped down behind her.

Soren.

He puffed out a misty breath in the icy stairwell. Held up a stick, thick as her forearm and almost as tall as she was, to explain his delay. A weapon.

At the back of the chamber, Rane let out a cry, and a rope of fear twisted through her. Eric held his staff in his right hand, a concentrated beam of blue light coming from the tip. Smoke rose up, and the acrid smell of burning cotton wafted across to her. Eric was burning Rane's back through his shirt.

The creature hanging in tandem with Rane lifted a weary head, and cried back in sympathy. The sound should have been pitiful, but instead was courageous, heart-wrenching.

Rane raised his head to acknowledge it. His eyes glittered in the torchlight.

She couldn't wait a moment longer.

She stood, lifted her hands, and yanked Eric's staff from his hands, her fear and panic sending it straight up to the ceiling, where it hit the rock with smack and then fell back down.

Soren took advantage of the distraction and ran along the wall, his stick raised.

A shudder rippled through her as she concentrated on the chains that held Rane and his fellow prisoner, and light flashed, cutting through the iron.

They both dropped.

Neither was expecting it, and they landed hard. Rane rolled off the table, but the creature lay where it was, too exhausted, in too much pain, to move.

"Help it," Kayla murmured to Sooty. Then she took a bold step forward.

Eric was staring at his empty hands in shock, then lunged for where his staff had landed on the ground. "It's cracked!"

The giant beside him pointed to her, then dived to grab Rane, hauled him up and held him tight.

"You!" Eric flinched, as if she'd struck him. "You were here all along. I knew you had to be."

Kayla ignored him, her attention on Rane.

He stopped struggling against the giant and lifted his head.

She stood for a beat, and then another, heart pounding as she looked into his eyes. At the absolute desolation there.

She felt a snap as her connection to wild magic was cut off. She spun, and watched the sphere wink out into nothing.

Their escape route had disappeared.

CHAPTER 31

*E*ric strode toward her, and she held out a hand to stop him, her fingers sparking.

The ball of wild magic at her shoulder spun so fast, it was a blur. Bringing it through had cut off their escape hatch, and she had the sinking feeling this was not enough. Not enough at all.

"How did you bring that in here?" Eric did stop, his gaze fixed on the sphere.

"It comes when I call." She wriggled her fingers, the purple green light at their tips shimmering.

"Wild magic doesn't answer to commands." There was a hitch in his voice, the first sign of uncertainty he'd shown.

Kayla ignored him, looked at the giant crushing Rane against its chest. She could see Rane struggling for breath, and she drew herself straighter, to do something—

Soren sprang from the shadows, so suddenly, so silently, she jumped in shock.

She'd forgotten about him, about his stealthy movement along the cave wall. They all had.

He brought his stick down on the giant's head, and it grunted, but didn't flinch. It turned its head to him, and he struck again, this time across its face.

A drop of blood, bright red against the green skin, trickled down the corner of its mouth.

It lifted Rane up and tossed him on the table. Lunged after Soren.

He leapt backward, stick striking out again. The giant advanced, unhurried.

Kayla swung her gaze back to the table, to Rane.

He was gone.

She looked for him in the shadows, and then she saw the gleam of blue. His blade.

The giant slammed a fist into Soren, and with a shout, he hit the wall and slid down it.

Eric did not move, did not look back. He ignored the fight behind him as if the result was a foregone conclusion. His gaze didn't waver from the wild magic sphere spinning at her shoulder.

The giant reached for Soren again and Rane struck. He brought the blade down from behind it, slicing into its back, and it bellowed, the sound a vibration that hurt her teeth.

With a wild flick of its arm, moving faster than seemed possible for something so large, the giant knocked Rane back. He landed on his back on the floor, and Kayla winced.

The giant turned from Soren, clutching at its wound awkwardly with one hand, the other making a fist, a hammer, to pound Rane into pieces.

Its fist went up, and Rane tried to move, to scramble away, but there was no way he could.

Like before with the asrai, panic and fear made Kayla draw more wild magic than she needed. It flashed through her, searing and alive, and the purple light that hit the giant was concentrated. Powerful. For a moment she was blind and deaf to everything, consumed by the light.

The giant stopped mid-swing, frozen. It toppled sideways, crashing into the table, smashing it as it went down. Its arm caught in the chains used to hang Rane and it landed with its torso raised off the ground, swinging wildly.

Blind-eyed. Dead.

Her hand went to her mouth, blood pounding in her ears. What was left of the ball of wild magic drifted forward. It was no bigger than her head.

She looked up and saw that Eric had at last turned to see what was behind him. He spun back to her, his face frozen in shock at what she'd done. He shook himself free of his stupor, and a light came in his eyes. Cunning and openly hungry. It snapped her back to herself.

"I thought I'd have an earth magic witch to command, but this is better. Much, much better."

RANE STARED AT HIS BROTHER. Somehow free, somehow here. Soren lay, winded and gasping on the floor, and Kayla stood, alone in the center of the room, drawing Eric's attention from them.

She had used up almost all her wild magic. He could see the little sphere left over spinning around her, a planet to her sun.

He knew now, without any doubt, he loved her. That he would die for her if he had to. Do whatever it took to get her out of here safely.

To his right, something moved, and he saw Sooty had finally nudged the creature Kayla had freed to the wall, and it had begun to pull itself up. It was the same kind as the creature Rane had met by the river, and he winced as he caught a glimpse of its ravaged back.

His own stung, a throbbing, burning pain, as if Eric was still at work on him. He could feel the line Eric had made as if it stood out like a ridge on his skin. Like some freakish abnormality.

He took a step toward Soren, held out his hand, and his brother grasped it, his hold stronger than Rane would have guessed from the look of him.

He was thin as a walking skeleton, his face haggard. He looked like a stranger and his eyes gave nothing away.

There was no time for talking. Rane turned back to Eric and Kayla, and pressed the dragon on the hilt of his knife again.

It was time to kill the sorcerer.

Eric seemed to sense his intent, because he moved, standing sideways so he could keep an eye on Kayla and Rane at the same time.

"You lied about my princess, I'm assuming you lied about my gem, too."

"Strapped to my back." Rane smiled. He reached his hand back, and felt . . . nothing. The gem was gone. He patted his shirt, keeping his smile confident for Eric. It must have slipped out when the stone giant had flicked him backwards.

"Good. Then I have the two things I want from you, De'Villier. I don't need you any more."

"Lift the enchantment, then." It was his one fear. That he'd kill the bastard and still be stuck with his twisted torture-spell.

Eric shrugged. "I lifted it already. Didn't you feel it as you came into the castle?"

Rane laughed. "Someone was kicking my head in. I didn't notice much else."

He saw Kayla tighten her fists. She kept her voice calm. "It's not like you to play fair, Eric."

His lips twisted in a sneer. "I couldn't have the enchantment active while I . . . dealt with De'Villier. It would have interfered with the other things I wanted to do."

"Lucky me."

Kayla frowned, her eyes going to the shadows behind Eric, and Rane remembered Soren.

Where was the idiot?

He attacked out of the gloom silently, swinging the thick stick at Eric, managing a glancing blow to his shoulder as the sorcerer leapt aside. There was a crack, wood hitting bone, and Eric cried out.

Not such an idiot.

Soren lifted back his stick to strike another blow at Eric's head. Eric lashed back, and Soren grunted as the sorcerer's staff tip caught him in the gut.

Rane circled the fight, knife out, his focus on Eric complete.

Eric moved, turning, keeping them both in view. He raised his staff, its tip glowing blue, but there was a long, thin crack in the wood that started at the top and ran down a third of its length. Blue light leaked from it, hemorrhaging power.

"Oh, no you don't." Kayla thrust her hands out.

Purple light flashed against blue, and Rane decided they were fighting for control over Eric's staff. He was clutching it, his face contorted with effort.

Rane circled the other way, to get behind the sorcerer and stab him in the back. Or cut his throat.

As he moved, something flashed on the floor in the light Kayla and Eric were generating.

The gem.

Both Kayla and Eric turned to look at it.

Eric did something, shoved Kayla back a few steps, and dived for it.

The bastard was going to get his hands on it, after all.

KAYLA REGAINED her balance from the magical shove Eric had given her, hands out and heart seizing in her chest at the thought of what would happen when Eric touched the gem.

But Soren must have seen it as well, seen Eric's wild lunge, because he dived for it, too.

"Soren! No!" He was going to sacrifice himself again.

He ignored her, or didn't hear her.

To one side, Rane bellowed a warning as Eric and Soren hit the floor together, hands out, and she ran to him. Best to be close.

Maybe Eric would get it first. Maybe . . .

The gem-light flared.

She threw her hands out, built a barrier of wild magic from where she stood beside Rane across the height and breadth of the dungeon.

Sooty was behind her.

Please, let Sooty still be behind her.

The gem pulsed a moment, and she could see Soren and Eric clearly silhouetted. Then it stopped, as abruptly as it had begun, and Kayla shuddered as the last of the wild magic coursed through her and cut off. Used up.

Eric was crouched low, a blue sheen of magic covering him like a turtle shell, his staff flashing strangely in his hands.

The gem winked in the torchlight where Soren had dropped it.

But Soren wasn't there any more.

CHAPTER 32

*T*he gem light shut off, and Kayla's wall collapsed.

Rane saw the last of her wild magic disappear, saw her flinch as it shrank to a minute point and wink out. Kayla had nothing left to use.

He turned back to where Soren had been, staring at the spot. The gem lay on the floor, glittering, deadly, and beside it, lay Soren's stick.

His brother was gone.

After everything, his brother was gone.

Eric moved, just to the side of him, pulling himself to his feet.

Rane felt as if the grindylow from the fog had slashed him open with its putrid claws. He looked across at Eric, and their eyes met.

Eric recoiled, stumbling back.

Rane felt strangely short of breath, strangely light-headed. He brought his knife up, felt a warm rush of satisfaction as Eric's gaze went to the blue glitter of the blade. He could hear nothing but a pounding in his ears, and his vision narrowed, darkening at the edges.

A scream, wild, feral, came from the stairs, and it was as if his earlier thought of the grindylow had conjured it up. It exploded into the room. Something had happened when he'd killed its mate. He must have snapped the control Eric had had over it.

And now he wished he hadn't because it went for the closest target.

Kayla.

Sooty charged forward, hissing, her back up, but there was no chance she could stop it, it was almost on Kayla—

It shrieked, arching its back, writhing in place. Rane felt white-hot pain along the line Eric had made in his back earlier, and from its place against the wall, the purple creature let out a thin, exhausted cry.

Rane had seen its back, and knew with a crushing certainty its pain was a hundred times worse than his own.

Rane forced his head right, toward Eric, and saw the sorcerer's staff glowed blue again. He was working a spell.

This was how he controlled his minions.

He imbedded something in their backs, and when he wanted to, he could bring them to their knees.

As Rane thought it, the grindylow did sink to its knees, keening, and then curled up on the floor, beyond sound.

Rane only had one welt across his own back, and still his knees dipped. He fought against it, fought to stand upright. He welcomed the pain, hoped Eric kept it up, ramped the agony up another notch. Because while he did, Kayla was safe.

He started walking to the grindylow, one foot-dragging step at a time. Sweat beaded on his forehead, on his upper lip, and he lifted an unsteady hand to wipe it away.

"Rane?" Kayla's call was soft, and even though he didn't think it wise, he looked at her, met her gaze.

She flinched at what she saw there. And he wondered whether it was his hatred of Eric or his pain that affected her.

Then he knew.

She turned to Eric with such rage, such focus, if there had been even the tiniest trace of wild magic in the air, Eric would have felt it.

She moved fast, scooping down to grab up Soren's stick, and he saw what she was going to do.

"Wait." It came out as a whisper, and he swallowed, worked some moisture back into his throat. All the while, Rane was getting closer, closer, to the grindylow. Eric needed to be conscious, needed to keep his spell going, for a little while longer.

She raised the stick up and back, getting ready to swing as she strode toward Eric, her face set.

"Wait." It was loud enough for her to hear this time, and she stopped short, her gaze flying to his.

Rane stood over the grindylow, fumbled with his knife, missing the dragon once, twice. Then he had it.

He dropped straight down. Let gravity do the work for him as he plunged the blade into the grindylow's neck.

The blood gushed and sprayed, covering him, but he couldn't move. Now he was down on the floor, the thought of rising, of moving at all, was impossible. He sank lower, rested his head on the stone paving.

He wanted to reach behind him and rip the skin from his back, flay himself to be rid of the agony.

The creature beside Sooty had long since fallen to the ground, half-unconscious with pain. Its eyes opened, and for a moment they stared at each other, at floor-level, and he felt a bond forged between them.

And then the pain was gone.

Kayla had broken the spell. Eric's hands were raised to protect his head, his staff on the floor, as Kayla brought back her stick for another blow. Blood poured from the side of his head.

He rolled out of Kayla's reach, grabbing his staff and holding it close to his body, like a ward against evil.

"I will have my marks on you." His mouth twisted and his eyes were narrow. "You will be mine."

He threw out his arm, circled his staff over his head. He must have planned to vanish, but the light was still leaking from the crack Kayla had made earlier and he only flickered in and out of sight.

Kayla took another swing at him, but before she could connect, at last his staff worked, and he disappeared.

Rane tried to pull himself up.

He was weighed down. The receding pain from Eric's spell, the bone-deep fatigue, the soul-deep sorrow over Soren. They held him in a grip stronger than two stone giants.

Then he turned to Kayla, and found her looking at him, the cool gray of her eyes calming, giving him strength. He reached out a hand to her and she helped him to his feet.

"Let's go."

CHAPTER 33

They staggered out of the castle, and Rane was glad all over again he had killed the second grindylow. Walking back into the mists around the castle would have been impossible if it had still been loose.

Sooty ranged around them, protective, sniffing the air, and by the look on her face, not liking what she smelled.

The purple creature from the dungeon was slung between Kayla and himself, its legs dragging from shin to toes on the ground behind them as they lurched down into the valley.

Kayla kept looking across at him, her teeth worrying her lower lip. "How far is the forest?"

"It's not that far. You'll see it when we get through those wells." His words were gasped, and he wasn't breathing properly.

She gave a nod and didn't speak again, putting her head down and taking the strain when she wasn't glancing across at him, to check on him.

She had saved him. Saved his brother, although typical Soren, he had refused to stay saved.

She was all he ever wanted.

When she looked across at him again he held her gaze, and her eyes softened.

After that, they both concentrated on getting away as fast as possible.

Even though the creature they were carrying was tall, it didn't weigh that much, not to him. It was starved and light-boned, and they got through the wells quicker than he thought they would.

The pain, the reaction from Eric's spell, started to lift, and it must have been doing the same for the creature they carried between them, because it lifted its head a little and gave a small sound of astonishment as they stepped through the wells and into the mist fields where the grindylows had hunted him.

Rane remembered the angle he had come in at, and nudged them in that direction, until suddenly, they were out of the mists and standing near the river where he'd washed earlier.

Dusk was only just setting, the late summer evening sky still orange and pink in the west.

The creature struggled a little, and Rane realized it was trying to stand on its own.

He and Kayla stopped and it slowly got its feet under it, and stood, hands on their shoulders to keep itself steady.

"What is your name?" Kayla asked it.

"Huri." It looked at the water, and then turned away, and something about the way it moved told Rane she was female.

"Are you from here, or did Eric bring you from somewhere else?" Kayla fitted herself more securely under Huri's arm.

Huri shook her head, her eyes averted from the river bank.

"I saw someone like you," Rane told her. "Earlier today."

As he spoke, a shadow rose up from the river bank, standing from a crouch.

It was the creature Rane had cut earlier, the white of the bandage stark against his purple skin.

Huri gave a quiet moan. It sounded to Rane like the final death throe of a tree, just after the last axe stroke.

She half-turned her back, her eyes down, her whole body shaking, and Rane moved away from her, letting Kayla take more of her weight, as he left himself free to protect them all.

Beside him, appearing so suddenly his heart skipped in a

moment of sheer terror, Sooty butted his hip, her lips drawn back in a snarl.

The creature he'd met earlier, clearly known to Huri, and of the same people, raised his hands in alarm, and looked over their shoulders, to where Eric's castle would be, if it wasn't hidden from sight.

"Bad gone?"

"For now," Rane said. "But he'll be back."

There was no way Eric would abandon his castle. He may have beaten a retreat, but he had too many magical things in the castle.

But not as many as he'd had.

Rane could feel the weight of the gem in his pouch. Along with a few other items that had called to him more strongly than the others in the dungeon, before they'd climbed the stairs and let themselves out.

Eric had lost this round.

But there was a war coming, and Rane knew the outcome was far from certain.

The creature before him suddenly called to Huri, in a language that sounded solely constructed of tongue clicks.

She turned away even more, twisting and hunching so she wouldn't have to look at him.

He spoke again, more urgently, and she shook her head.

"What does he want, Huri?" Kayla looked between them, and Rane could see she was upset by the situation.

"He wants to understand why I hurt him. Tried to kill him. Didn't want Eric to have him, like me."

"Eric wanted you to bring him in, and you tried to kill him instead, so he wouldn't become another of Eric's slaves?"

She nodded. "Tried to tell him to run. He wouldn't. Grindylow coming. Stone giant coming." She made a gesture, a cut along her leg, and Rane's gaze went back to the creature's scar he'd seen earlier that day.

"What's your name?" he asked him.

"Ker." He looked between Sooty and Rane, and Rane wondered if he was considering his chances of fighting them.

"Do you understand what Huri is saying? That in order to stop you being made into Eric's puppet like she had been, she tried to kill you instead?" Kayla stepped even closer to Huri, put her arms around her, and Rane realized Huri was close to collapse.

"Let's talk about it on the way to the forest. I don't think Huri can last much longer." He stepped closer to Huri as well, and got her arm over his shoulder.

"Thought there no choice. But was wrong. Ker is alive. Fine." Huri's voice was soft, shamed.

They started moving again, with Sooty closer to them, now, and Ker trailing in their wake, keeping a cautious distance.

The forest was right ahead, and Rane could see a strange glow coming from it. Like it was lit with purple lanterns.

Kayla seemed to move faster, the closer they got, and when they were on the same level as the trees, and could at last see between the trunks, Rane jerked them all to a halt.

There was a sentinel line of wild magic spheres waiting for them, the line stretching as far as his eye could see in both directions.

"What is this about?" he asked Kayla, looking at her over Huri's bowed head.

She took a moment to answer. In the end, she shrugged. "A homecoming welcome."

THEY MADE their camp in the thin trees at the forest's edge. Wild magic circled them, a fence that no-one would be foolish enough to try to breach.

Just being near them made Kayla feel better. Stronger.

Ker had hesitated at the sight, and then stepped in with them, had allowed himself to be included in the protected area.

He sat a little away from the fire Rane had started, though, as if he had no welcome with them, although Kayla and Rane had both asked him to join them.

Huri was either unconscious or asleep where they had lain her down.

Rane sat staring into the fire light, and Kayla reached out a hand and touched his shoulder. "I'm sorry about Soren. So, so sorry."

He turned to look at her slowly. "How did you get him out?"

"I broke into Jasper's stronghold, healed him with the apple, and then managed to trick Jasper into bringing us up above ground. I used wild magic to get us away."

She thought how ridiculous it was that so much fear and exertion could be summed up into so few words.

Rane reached over and took her arm. Gently turned it over to look at her wrist.

He circled it with his fingers, tilted it so the firelight illuminated it. The fine pattern was denser, far more intricate, than it had been before.

She hadn't looked at it since Nuen had grabbed her arm in Jasper's stronghold, and she gasped. "It's . . . beautiful."

It was a delicate spiral; airy, light and detailed. It reached a handspan from her wrist up her inner arm.

She sensed Rane's frown.

"You don't think so?"

"No, it's not that." He rubbed a thumb over the markings. "I feel . . . nervous when I look at it. That it is taking you from me, marking you as its own."

"It feels like the other way around." She touched it lightly with her fingers. "Like I am marking it. Shaping it."

"Why does it need you? Why does it let you use it?" He looked up at the wild magic around them. "Are they hemming us in, or protecting us?"

"Protecting. No doubt about it." She withdrew her arm. "But sometimes protection can be misguided. Like leaving someone without talking about it, to keep them safe." She had considered letting this conversation go. It was done. There was no changing that he'd left her and chosen for them both. She even understood why he had done it, but she would not let it happen again.

He lifted his head, and held her gaze. "If you'd come with me, the golden apple and the gem would be in Eric's hands and we would both be under his control."

She gave a nod. "I don't dispute it. But we should have discussed it. Made a plan of action. You chose to make the decision on your own."

"I wanted you safe." He ran a hand through his hair, and looked across at Ker, hunched miserably over himself a little way away.

"I know. I don't care." She looped her arms over her knees and hugged them tight. "If it affects us both, if either one of us could be in danger, we have to talk about it."

He waited a long time before he answered. She preferred it that way. It meant he'd really thought about it.

"All right. In future, we talk about it." It was an admission of so much more than how he would treat her from now on. It was an admission of the fact that they were a team.

They were together.

"Good." She smoothed a hand over his shoulder, her hand trembling at the enormity of the shift in how things were.

He looked at her in the firelight, and opened his mouth to speak just as Huri sat up with a scream.

They both scrambled to their feet, and she saw Ker rising as well, his attention riveted on Huri.

Huri dragged herself to her feet, looking through the trees, toward the field that held Eric's castle.

"I didn't think he'd come back so quickly," Rane said, pulling out his knife. His other hand went up to touch his back, and his face was white and drawn, like it had been during the grindylow attack in the dungeon.

"Perhaps he's not welcome anywhere else." Kayla was quite sure he wasn't.

Then Huri started walking toward the tree line, her face so haunted, so fill of agony, Kayla drew a wild magic sphere to her without even thinking about it.

"Huri, can I try to stop this? Stop the pain?"

Huri tripped on something, a root or a stick, and fell heavily.

She lay for a moment, and then started to pull herself along the floor with her elbows. "Stop?"

"I will try. Will you let me?"

She nodded, but kept dragging herself toward Eric.

Kayla lifted her hands and hesitated. She would love to have Ylana here with her, helping her, telling her what to do.

But she didn't, and every second she wasted, Huri was getting closer to Eric.

She imagined Huri's back, smooth and unharmed, imagined her without pain.

Purple flared from her hands, but it was met with a flare of blue wherever it touched Huri, a vicious spark that threw her into even more pain. Her cries made Kayla physically sick.

She drew back, and smoke was coming off of Huri, the stench of it like manure burning.

Ker shoved her, clicking and shouting in her face, and she raised her hands.

"There must be a protective spell on top of the other magic."

She pushed him aside and crouched next to Huri, but she was unconscious now, the cry that had cut Kayla all the way through her heart was the last sound she'd made.

"Take her." Rane stepped beside Kayla, standing over her with his gaze on Ker. "Take Huri. Put her over your shoulder and run as far from here as you can. I don't think he can hurt her, or compel her if you're far enough away."

Ker looked at them, at the wild magic, and then beyond, through the trees toward where Eric's castle lay. He bent and Rane helped him lift Huri up, draping her over his shoulder.

"As far as you can go," Rane told him, and Kayla thought he wanted to do the same.

Ker grunted and then turned, and Kayla waved a hand, so the wild magic parted and moved to form a purple-lit path away from the forest edge.

His first few steps were unsteady, and then he found his rhythm and he was gone, Huri limp as a puppet down his back.

"Do you want me to try on you?" Kayla lifted a hand to her

throat, because she didn't know if she had the stomach to try again. "I watched him mark you, and I don't think he'd finished before I interrupted. There might not be any protection over his marks on you."

Rane lifted a hand to his back again. "I saw you pull back when Huri screamed like that. I think that's when you should have gone harder, punched all the way through. Even if I beg you to stop, that's what I want you to do to me."

"What if you pass out, like Huri?" Kayla waited as he looked away.

She didn't want to do this at all. But she would.

Her hands trembled, but she bunched them into fists.

Rane ran a finger along his back. "I would rather die than let Eric have any power over me."

She drew in a breath, wanting to tell him she would never let that happen, but after a moment gave a nod. Not in agreement, but in acknowledgment of his wishes.

The wild magic sphere she had called to her to help Huri was still hovering just over her shoulder and she held out her hands and closed her eyes.

She touched him with wild magic, felt the flare as Eric's spell tried to counter it.

Rane cried out as blue and purple clashed, and with horror, she saw him fall down to his knees.

CHAPTER 34

*R*ane was free again.

It came at a price. He felt a strange tingle across his shoulders, like the skin was numbed, but whether it was temporary or permanent, he didn't care.

Eric's power was gone.

Kayla was kneeling right next to him, cupping his face in his hands, and he drew her to him in the first real embrace he had given her since she'd come to rescue him from the castle.

"You're all right?"

"I'm all right." He smiled against her cheek. "It looks like there wasn't a protective spell."

She sagged against him, and they stayed that way, in each others' arms, until at last they grew stiff and uncomfortable.

"Let's move deeper into the forest," he said, "I don't like how close we are to the edge."

She gave a nod, and he almost laughed at what he'd just said. Getting deeper into the forest had always been the last thing he'd wanted to do. Now he saw it as the safest option.

He kicked sand on the fire, and picked up the saddlebags Kayla and Soren had brought through the wild magic doorway. One looked familiar.

"Where did you get this?"

"The clearing near Jasper's stronghold. Soren says they belonged to the men out hunting you." Kayla took up one as well.

"It belonged to an old friend of mine. Someone I trained with as a knight for Jasper. He captured me on my way to Eric. And then he touched the gem."

She shivered. "Even before I knew you'd been there, and they had been caught in the gem's magic, I felt a darkness there. What do you think happens to them? Where do you think they go?"

He shrugged. "I haven't stopped thinking about it since Soren disappeared. No place good, if they go anywhere. Maybe they simply die."

She looked at him a moment, and then turned away, started walking into the forest. She clicked her tongue, and Sooty was suddenly beside her, and he watched them both, elegant, sleek, as they moved in unison.

She wasn't the same woman who had started this journey with him, and he wasn't the same either.

He started after them, and from behind him, he thought he heard a faint scream.

He looked over his shoulder, but there was nothing but the thin tree line and the field beyond.

And enough wild magic to make anything Eric sent after them think twice before setting foot into the forest.

THEY LAY at last beside the fire, no longer hungry or cold.

Sooty was prowling off somewhere in the trees, and the gentle bob and weave of wild magic lit their camp in a surreal glow.

"I never thought I would relax because I was surrounded by wild magic." Rane's voice was bemused. "It was the one thing both Soren and I hated and feared for so long."

"I don't know why it lets me command it. It is almost as if it is lonely, or in need of someone to direct it. And I know there is more I could do."

"Do you have to know everything?" Rane pulled her closer to him, and she heard the steady beat of his heart against her ear.

"If there is a war coming, and I can fight against Eric and his fellow sorcerers, then I want to know everything. I think I'll have to go back to Ylana. I understand so much more since I enchanted her. I need to release her and beg her to help me."

Rane tensed beside her, his eyes flashing. "No."

"This isn't over, Rane." Kayla lay back down, watching the purple light play off the muscles of his throat and shoulders. "Jasper has the golden apple, and—"

"What?" He reared up, towered over her.

She forced herself to relax. "Soren was holding it when Nuen hit him with a flash of magic. It saved his life, but he dropped it when he fell."

"So Nuen is healed, now?" Rane's eyes glittered in the firelight, and she almost couldn't meet his gaze.

"Yes. Soren wanted to go back for it, but I wouldn't let him. I could barely contain Nuen as it was, because I was outside the forest, and only able to get the wild magic in thin ribbons of power. I didn't have enough strength to take him on if he was fully healed."

He looked like a man in a struggle, fighting a dozen angry demons. He closed his eyes. Took a deep breath. "You could have been killed, Kayla. Nuen could have killed you."

She held his gaze. "He could have. But the truth is, if I had had more power, I could have killed him, too. I was just as dangerous. More, because he was weak and ill."

"He isn't weak and ill any more." Rane's tone was tired. Weary.

She drew him down, and he curved his arm around her shoulders. "With the golden apple, we can be sure Nuen is fit again. And Eric is out there, and he hates us more than ever."

"Hates me." Rane's mouth curved into a humorless smile. "Wants you even more." His grip on her tightened.

"Why, though?" She looked down at her hands. "He wanted me

before he knew I could use wild magic. Was it only because he knew I was a witch, or because I was a witch *and* the princess of Gaynor? If we knew that, maybe we could understand what is going on."

"I don't think he's the type to have told anyone his plans."

"My father knows something. Or that's the way it seemed to me. Although not everything. There were definitely secrets between him and Eric." Kayla looked up at him, watched his face turn stubborn. "And Ylana will know."

He shook his head, but she refused to let it drop.

"If any one does, it's her." She touched her wrist again. "She can help us."

"She won't."

"Maybe not. But we have the gem. Perhaps we can return it, gain her forgiveness. Or maybe her hatred for the sorcerers is bigger than her anger at us."

Rane was shaking his head, but she knew she was right. "When I spoke with her, she sounded tired. Tired of doing everything on her own. If we offer to help—"

"I will not be Ylana's helper." Rane's mouth was a grim line.

"I will." She spoke quietly, determined. "I'll risk it."

He lifted a hand to her shoulder, gripped her. "I don't want you at risk. I dragged you into this . . ."

"No." She pressed a finger to his lips. "Eric would have taken me that day if I hadn't helped you with the apple. I would be his now. I would have welts on my back."

She saw him accept what she said. Saw the pain in his eyes lessen.

"I want to hide you away. Out of Eric's grasp." He moved over her, supporting his weight with one arm, cupping her cheek with his other hand.

"I can't hide." She moved so close to him she could feel his heat, searing her through his shirt and hers. Could smell the salt and wood-smoke on his skin. "I don't think anyone can. Whatever is coming will affect the whole of Middleland."

He stroked his thumb over her lip. "Yes."

"What will you do?" She lifted her hand, slid it behind his neck.

"Protect you."

She held his gaze. "You can't do that. I am going to Ylana."

"Kayla." He bent his head, rested his forehead on hers. "I won't let you go to Ylana alone. I'll come with you."

"She holds some of the answers. It will be worth it." She threaded her fingers in the hair at his nape.

"Worth dying for?" He shook his head. Shrugged with resignation. "We can go to Ylana. And if she agrees to help us, then, after . . ." He drew back, his eyes dark and cold as the dungeon they'd climbed out of to escape Eric's castle. "I'll hunt Eric down. And take Jasper down with him."

She wanted to beg him not to. To beg him to stay as safe as he wanted her, but she said nothing. Out of nowhere, tears welled in her eyes and she blinked them away, biting down on her lip to stop it trembling.

"Shh. What is it?"

For the first time ever, she saw panic on his face.

"I love you."

He froze. She was so close to him, she saw his pupils retract in shock. Then he relaxed. Traced a tear down her cheek and flicked it away. "I know."

She suddenly saw what she was looking for in his eyes. Saw everything she needed.

She let her hand slip down, over his collarbone to his heart. Felt it race beneath her palm.

"I love you, too." He bent his head to whisper in her ear, and pulled her even closer.

She lay quiet in his arms.

They had challenges ahead. So much was unresolved or still a mystery. And the stakes were higher than she ever could have imagined.

But lying under the trees of the forest, in the wild heart of Middleland, she knew whatever lay ahead, she and Rane would face it together.

And it would be all right.

THE SILVER PEAR

The Golden Apple is followed by The Silver Pear.

About The Silver Pear:
An unlikely princess . . .
Kayla is determined to master her new-found abilities as a wild magic witch. She's learning everything she can so she and her betrothed, Rane, can put a stop to the sorcerers who are recklessly gathering their power, building up their magic to take each other on in a war that will destroy the countries of Middleland.
An even more unlikely sorcerer . . .
Mirabelle's father was one of the greatest sorcerers in Middleland, but when he used the magic in the silver pear to bespell his pregnant wife to give birth to the greatest sorcerer who would ever live, he never thought that child would be a girl. Mirabelle is nothing like a usual sorcerer, confounding every expectation, and when she comes to the rescue of Rane's brother, Soren, she makes a decision few sorcerers would. She saves him, rather than herself, losing the silver pear in the process.
And using magic always exacts a price . . .
With war not just a possibility but simply a matter of time, there

are no neutral parties and no fence-sitters in Kayla and Mirabelle's new world. Everyone is either an ally or an enemy and there is a price to pay for everything. The question is, how high will it be?

EXCERPT: THE SILVER PEAR

66 *Soren and Mirabelle*

*S*oren's hand slammed down on the glittering gem lying on Eric's dungeon floor a split second before Eric got to it, and he was flung, hard and fast as a stone from a catapult, into blinding darkness. His shout was ripped from his throat, and air pounded against his ears, deafening him.

He felt as if the howling winds would tear his limbs from his body, and he curled in on himself protectively.

As suddenly as it began, the wind stopped. The quiet, the darkness, the lack of pressure, made him think for a moment he had died.

Then he began to fall.

It felt like forever, but he realized as he hit the ground it could only have been a six foot drop. He rolled as he made contact—hard, rain-slicked cobbles digging into his skin as he spun.

When he came to a stop against a wall, he had to wait for the dizziness to pass before he sat up.

The legs of a man were before him. Slowly, his gaze travelled up to a pocked, grey face.

"Well, well, well." The man stared at him for a moment, then turned. "Baldic, looks like we've another for the collection."

"Collection?" Soren began pushing against the wall, trying to stand. "Where am I?"

The man laughed. "That's what they all ask." He stepped back, waited for Soren to gain his feet, then he lunged forward, pinning Soren to the wall with a pitch- fork, the tines just wide enough to accommodate a man's neck.

Soren fought it, the metal cutting into his throat, choking him.

He'd been restrained too recently, and for too long, to accept that treatment again. Whatever this place was, his welcome boded ill, and the thought of another cell, another round of torture and captivity, made him wild.

He had only escaped from Jasper a few days ago, had barely come to terms with his new freedom.

He would not give it up.

He threw himself forward, and the man had to shove back using all his strength.

There were lights dancing in front of his eyes. He needed to stop fighting or he'd choke, but he could not. Would not. Not again.

He saw tiny spots of bright, colored light, and felt his body slide down the wall. The pressure on his throat eased a little, and he lay, panting for breath.

"This one needs extra watching." The man turned, speaking to someone just beside him. Then he swung back, spoke clearly into Soren's ear. "Welcome to Halakan."

A LIGHT FLARED over the Halakan stronghold. Blue and bright.

Miri saw it through her window and shivered, her hand going up to grasp the silver pear hanging from the cord around her neck.

She felt the tingle of its magic against her fingertips, and loosened her grip.

The guard outside her door shifted uneasily in a creak of leather as he saw the light, too. She heard the second guard, whose turn it was to do a perimeter check, walk faster around the corner than usual.

"Hope it's not as many coming through as last time." The guard spoke to his companion softly, but she could hear him easily enough.

Last time the light flared, two days ago, it had deposited five men into the Halakan stronghold at once. The most it ever had at one time.

The arrival of so many had finally pushed William of Nesta to her door personally. His written summons and her polite refusals were clearly no longer an option.

He had tried to cajole, then bribe, then threaten her to question the men.

When she'd refused, things had taken an . . . interesting turn.

William had gotten his own way for too long. He was rusty in dealing with someone who wouldn't obey him.

She'd seen the regret in his eyes as he'd surrounded her house, unable to call back his threats. He'd been forced to follow through or lose face.

As she'd shut her door in deliberate disdain, there'd been a catch of nerves on his lips as they pursed together, perhaps as he wondered if he'd pushed her too far.

After all, he knew she was powerful. That was why he was asking for her help.

So far, the stand-off had settled into him posting guards outside her house, but soon she'd have to step outside. She hadn't the cupboard stores to withstand a long siege.

She was down to the last of her food. A day, two at most, and she would start to go hungry.

She wondered what William would do then. What *she* would do.

Did he have a plan for when she became desperate?

As it was, he hadn't dared use his knights to break into her house and bring her out by force.

Was he afraid of what she would do to them, or was he afraid to test their loyalty too far?

Interesting question.

But regardless of the answer, the time had come to act. The light had flashed again, which meant at least one more stranger had mysteriously appeared in the stronghold, and only two days after the last time.

If she didn't do something, William would be back again, a little more forceful, a little more desperate, and she refused to cave to his demands.

If she showed even the slightest hint of weakness there were other sorcerers who might decide it would be worth the risk to take her on. To make a deal with William he couldn't refuse.

Up until now she'd had what her father had called the dragon's advantage.

She was so mysterious, so cloaked in rumor and myth, no one was prepared to challenge her.

If she allowed William to bully her, the veil would be stripped away, and she would be revealed.

Not that she was bluffing. She was powerful enough. But she didn't want to be dragged into the insidious power game that had begun four years ago, and had slowly escalated.

She'd been too young to even be considered a threat when it started; when Eric the Bold and Hirst Red Tongue had openly fought with each other at the closing banquet of a sorcerers' gathering.

There had always been jealousies and back-biting aplenty, but there were strict rules directing behavior. That night, neither Eric nor Hirst had bothered with them. And when Hirst had died, and Eric had taken Hirst's staff and helped himself to the golden apple, Hirst's prize possession—given, it was rumored, to Hirst's great-grandfather by a grateful goddess—others had begun to wonder what they might help themselves to, if they did the same.

She shook her head to focus on the present, and went into her bedroom, pulling off the gown she wore and taking out the men's clothing she'd collected through the years.

Her father had taken on apprentices in the beginning, over and over again trying to deny what she was, what she had to become.

The young men had never been good enough, according to him. Staying four months, sometimes six. Jack had been the longest-lasting, almost a year he'd stayed, and in that time, outgrown more than one set of clothes.

She pulled on his old trousers, and was relieved to find they fit her well enough. The shirt was too big, but she cinched it around her waist with one of her own wide belts, and pulled on stockings and boots. The apprentice's old jacket was warm, if a little long in the arms for her, and she buttoned it up, although summer still had a hold on the forest.

The guards were talking to each other in low tones outside. The appearance of the blue light again so soon after the last time had stirred them up.

She walked through to the back of the house, hoping there wasn't a third guard she didn't know about, and opened the window. She pulled a tiny bit of magic from the silver pear to muffle the sounds she made climbing through, and dropped quietly into her back garden.

It had been raining earlier, a soft, gentle shower, and she used the magic in the silver pear again to wipe the footprints she'd made in the flowerbed away, and a little more to close the window silently behind her.

She had almost reached the wood that surrounded her house when one of the guards remembered about the perimeter check again, and by the time he came round, eyes on the house, not the garden or trees, she was well hidden.

She waited for him to turn the corner of her small house, pretty as a picture under the light of a moon ringed in silver by the last of the rain clouds, and took the path toward Halakan.

She'd been avoiding this. Avoiding using any magic at all. But since her father had disappeared two months ago, when she'd been gripped by the certainty of his death a month later, she'd known it was coming.

She couldn't balance on the fence any longer.

DARK HORSE

If you love speculative fiction, you may love Michelle Diener's award-winning Class 5 series. The series begins with DARK HORSE, book 1 in the Class 5 series.

ABOUT DARK HORSE:

Rose McKenzie may be far from Earth with no way back, but she's made a powerful ally--a fellow prisoner with whom she's formed a strong bond. Sazo's an artificial intelligence. He's saved her from captivity and torture, but he's also put her in the middle of a conflict, leaving Rose with her loyalties divided.

Captain Dav Jallan doesn't know why he and his crew have stumbled across an almost legendary Class 5 battleship, but he's not going to complain. The only problem is, all its crew are dead, all except for one strange, new alien being.

She calls herself Rose. She seems small and harmless, but less and less about her story is adding up, and Dav has a bad feeling his crew, and maybe even the four planets, are in jeopardy. The Class 5's owners, the Tecran, look set to start a war to get it back and Dav suspects Rose isn't the only alien being who survived what happened on the Class 5. And whatever else is out there is playing its own games.

In this race for the truth, he's going to have to go against his leaders and trust the dark horse.

Find out more at www.michellediener.com.

ALSO BY MICHELLE DIENER

SCIENCE FICTION NOVELS

Sky Raiders series:

Intended (Short Story Prequel Available Free to Newsletter Subscribers)

Sky Raiders

Calling the Change

Shadow Warrior

Class 5 series:

Dark Horse

Dark Deeds

Dark Minds

Dark Matters

Dark Ambitions: A Class 5 Novella

Dark Class

Dark Class Epilogue: Free on newsletter signup

Collision Course

Collision Course Epilogue: Free on newsletter signup

Verdant String series:

Interference & Insurgency Box Set

Breakaway

Breakeven

Trailblazer

High Flyer

Wave Rider

Peace Maker

Enthraller

Defender

FANTASY NOVELS BY MICHELLE DIENER

The Rising Wave series:

The Rising Wave (Prequel novella to THE TURNCOAT KING)

The Turncoat King

The Threadbare Queen

Fate's Arrow

Truth's Blade

Truth's Blade Bonus Short Story (Available free to newsletter subscribers)

Mistress of the Wind

The Dark Forest series:

The Golden Apple

The Silver Pear

HISTORICAL FICTION NOVELS

Traffic Warden Mysteries:

Ticket Out

Return Ticket

Susanna Horenbout series:

In a Treacherous Court

Dangerous Sanctuary (A short story - available for free, exclusively to readers who sign up to Michelle Diener's New Release Notification List)

Keeper of the King's Secrets

In Defense of the Queen

Regency London series:
The Emperor's Conspiracy
Banquet of Lies
A Dangerous Madness

Other historical novels:
Daughter of the Sky

SHORT PARANORMAL FICTION

Breaking Out: Part I (Short story)
Breaking Out: Part II (Novella)

To receive notification when a new book is released, sign up at michelledi
ener.com.

ACKNOWLEDGMENTS

Thanks as always to my critique partners, Edie and Kim, and to everyone who read or worked on the manuscript and gave some input. You all helped make this a better book. Thanks to Laura Morrigan for the amazing cover.

The Golden Apple is my second fairy tale retelling, in this case very loosely based on the Norwegian fairy tale The Princess on the Glass Hill.

ABOUT THE AUTHOR

Michelle Diener is an award winning author of historical fiction, science fiction and fantasy romance.

Michelle was born in London and currently lives in Australia with her husband and children.

You can contact Michelle through her website or sign up to receive notification when she has a new book out on her New Release Notification page.

Connect with Michelle
www.michellediener.com